*Ryan watched Emma nestle the baby
against her, her love obvious
to all of them.*

Emma was going to be a wonderful mother.

The baby suddenly opened her eyes, and Ryan would swear she was staring at him. It was the first time she'd been awake in his presence. It was all he could do to hold back an exclamation. The nurse pushed Emma and the baby to the car as he followed.

Almost like a family.

He gently placed the baby in the seat and belted her in. Without saying anything, he lifted Emma as easily as he had the baby and settled her in the front seat. Her gasp told him he'd surprised her.

"You did that well for a new daddy," the nurse said cheerfully.

But he heard Emma gasp. She knew he'd once had a child….

Dear Reader,

The year is off to a wonderful start in Silhouette Romance, and we've got some of our best stories yet for you right here.

Our tremendously successful ROYALLY WED series continues with *The Blacksheep Prince's Bride* by Martha Shields. Our intrepid heroine—a lady-in-waiting for Princess Isabel—will do anything to help rescue the king. Even marry the single dad turned prince! And Judy Christenberry returns to Romance with *Newborn Daddy*. Poor Ryan didn't know what he was missing, until he looked through the nursery window....

Also this month, Teresa Southwick concludes her much-loved series about the Marchetti family in *The Last Marchetti Bachelor*. And popular author Elizabeth August gives us *Slade's Secret Son*. Lisa hadn't planned to tell Slade about their child. But with her life in danger, there's only one man to turn to....

Carla Cassidy's tale of love and adventure is *Lost in His Arms*, while new-to-the-Romance-line Vivienne Wallington proves she's anything but a beginning writer in this powerful story of a man *Claiming His Bride*.

Be sure to come back next month for Valerie Parv's ROYALLY WED title as well as new stories by Sandra Steffen and Myrna Mackenzie. And Patricia Thayer will begin a brand-new series, THE TEXAS BROTHERHOOD.

Happy reading!

Mary-Theresa Hussey

Mary-Theresa Hussey
Senior Editor

Please address questions and book requests to:
Silhouette Reader Service
U.S.: 3010 Walden Ave., P.O. Box 1325, Buffalo, NY 14269
Canadian: P.O. Box 609, Fort Erie, Ont. L2A 5X3

Newborn Daddy

JUDY CHRISTENBERRY

SILHOUETTE *Romance*®
Published by Silhouette Books
America's Publisher of Contemporary Romance

SILHOUETTE BOOKS

ISBN 0-373-19511-7

NEWBORN DADDY

Visit Silhouette at www.eHarlequin.com

Printed in U.S.A.

Books by Judy Christenberry

Silhouette Romance

*The Lucky Charm Sisters
†The Circle K Sisters

JUDY CHRISTENBERRY

has been writing romances for over fifteen years because she loves happy endings as much as her readers do. She's a bestselling writer for Harlequin American Romance, but she has a long love of traditional romances and is delighted to tell a story that brings those elements to the reader. A former high school French teacher, Judy now devotes her time to writing. She hopes readers have as much fun reading her stories as she does writing them. She spends her spare time reading, watching her favorite sports teams and keeping track of her two adult daughters.

It's a bouncing baby girl!

Andrea.

Six pounds and one ounce/Nineteen inches

Mother is Emma Davenport

Notification of father pending...

but rumor has it it's Ryan Nix....

Chapter One

Ryan Nix stared at the newborn babies in the local hospital. He wouldn't be here if his sister, Beth, hadn't just given birth. Normally he avoided babies since his own child, Ryan, Jr., as well as his wife, Merilee, had died three years ago.

But he had to admit, his nephew was a fine-looking boy.

A nurse entered the nursery carrying a pink bundle. A girl. He was about to turn back to his nephew when the nurse put the baby girl in the bed next to Beth's baby. Then she slid the birth card into place. As she moved away, after smiling at him, he let his gaze drift to the birth card, not really reading it until he saw familiar words.

His name. Listed as the father.

Ryan got a sick feeling in his stomach. His gaze immediately shifted to the corresponding blank. Mother: Emma Davenport.

He slapped his hands on the glass wall for support and stared at the card, sure he'd misread it. What it said couldn't be true. There had to be another Ryan Nix.

Another Ryan Nix who'd had an affair with another Emma Davenport that had ended seven months ago.

Yeah, right.

Damn her, he'd told her he'd never have another child, never marry again. Hadn't she listened? In fact, he'd been downright rude, his anger raw and painful. She'd thought she could replace Merilee? Give him a child as perfect as Ryan Junior? Replace his lost family?

He'd sent her away, ended their affair, had nothing to do with her since.

Without thinking, he hurried back to the nurses' desk. "What room is Emma Davenport in?" he demanded.

"Two-twelve, sir," the nurse said. She appeared ready to add something else, but Ryan didn't wait. Her room was on the opposite side of the small hospital from Beth's.

His cowboy boots weren't quiet as he raced down the hall, but he was beyond consideration for anyone. He felt betrayed, and he was going to let the betrayer know about it.

He entered the room, his roar already in full force. "Emma Davenport!"

A pale face, smaller than he remembered, lay on the pillow. Alarm registered in her eyes by the time he paused.

"How dare you?" he ripped. "I told you I never wanted children! Did you think I was lying? Did you think you'd force me into marriage this way?"

He frowned when she didn't say a word. In fact, she'd closed her eyes.

"Emma! Did you hear me?"

The door opened. "I suspect everyone heard you, Mr. Nix," an older nurse, one who'd been a friend of his mother's, said. "Would you please step outside?"

"No! I want some answers!" he insisted, glaring at Emma. Then he frowned. If anything, Emma's pale face had whitened even more. Before he could express concern, however, the nurse had taken him by the arm.

"I think you'd better leave. Our patient needs her rest."

"Emma!" Ryan demanded.

"Please go." Her voice was barely a whisper, not the low, musical tones that had first attracted him.

Before he could protest or question Emma again, the nurse dragged him out into the hallway.

"Ryan, whatever issues you have with Miss Davenport, save them. She's having a difficult time and needs all her energy to get better."

"What do you mean?" Ryan asked, staring at the nurse. He remembered how pale Emma was. How she didn't respond. How her voice sounded sad and lifeless. "What's wrong with her?"

"Men!" the nurse exclaimed. "She just had a baby! Now, stay out of that room, or I'll call the doctor."

Ryan stumbled down the hallway, confused, still angry but worried. He walked by the nursery again, on the way to Beth's room, and he stopped to look at the child that was purportedly claimed to be his.

How could that tiny form be partly his? Even when Ryan, Jr. was small, he hadn't been *that* small. Or that delicate. Beautiful. Like Emma.

He cringed. He'd hidden from his behavior seven months ago when—*seven months*. Horrified, he took a deep breath and leaned against the wall. She'd been pregnant when she'd suggested—when she'd asked about moving in, about making a family. She'd already been pregnant.

And he'd yelled at her. Sent her away.

His mama had raised him to be a gentleman. But he hadn't been that day. He'd enjoyed Emma's body. He'd even admit to enjoying Emma. She was different from Merilee. His wife had been vibrant, alive, always the center of everything.

Emma was quiet, even shy at times. He'd sensed in her the same kind of wrenching loneliness he felt. He'd thought she'd understand why he wanted nothing personal, nothing permanent. But he hadn't told her. He hadn't been honest…but then she hadn't asked.

When he'd savaged her after her hesitant suggestion, it had never occurred to him that she might already be pregnant. He was ashamed of what he'd done. Had even considered apologizing, but he hadn't wanted her to hope he'd change his mind. Better for her to put him behind her and move on.

But she couldn't.

Because she was already pregnant.

"Damn!" he muttered.

"Ryan? That you? Are you admiring my son? Isn't he—?" His brother-in-law, Jack Kirby, broke off. "Shoot, I'm sorry, Ryan. I was so excited I forgot—I mean, uh, are you coming in to see Beth?"

"Yeah," Ryan agreed, his throat raw, his voice heavy. "That's what I was coming to do." He hurried toward Jack.

Jack led the way into Beth's room. His sister was smiling, and Jack immediately hurried to her side, hugging and kissing her before he pointed out Ryan's presence. "Hey, honey, look who's here?"

"Oh, Ryan, I'm so glad you came. Did you see him? Isn't he beautiful?" Beth asked, her face lit with happiness.

All Ryan could see was Emma's pale face, the sadness in her eyes. He looked around Beth's room. The rooms were identical, but Beth's was already filled with flowers...and a loving husband.

Emma had nothing.

Acid ate at his stomach. Guilt filled him. Emma had been alone for the past seven months. He knew because Beth had gone to see her after she and Ryan had split up. Beth had wanted to tell her they could still be friends, because she'd liked Emma. But Emma had refused, telling Beth it would be too painful.

He had occasionally asked Beth, or other women in town, about Emma, in a casual way. But she was like a shadow, barely appearing, slipping away, always bundled up.

Hiding her pregnancy.

"Ryan? Is it too hard for you? You can go home if it is. I appreciate you making the effort, but I'll understand." Beth offered him a gentle smile, putting aside her own happiness with concern for him.

He leaned over and kissed her cheek. "No, honey, I'm okay. You have a fine son. You have a right to be proud."

Both new parents beamed at him.

"Have you called Mom and Dad yet?" he asked.

"Oh, yes, I just talked to them. They're packing now. Dad even offered to fly Mom in, but she insisted she had to drive with him to make sure he didn't get lost," Beth said with a giggle. Their parents had retired to Florida shortly after Beth's wedding two years ago.

"When will you go home?" He figured since both babies were born the same day, Emma would go home then, too.

"Either tomorrow or Thursday. The doctor said it depends on how we're doing. Ryan, you didn't mind that I—we named him after you, did you?" Beth's pretty face crinked with a frown, watching him.

He worked hard to look pleased. "No, honey, I was proud. Ryan Jackson is a fine name. Of course, old Jackson here probably wanted his name first, but I'm better than him, so…" As he'd expected, Jack protested, taking his sister's attention away from him.

When they relaxed again, he said, "Uh, listen, I've got to go. Do you mind? Is there anything you need?"

"Oh, no, Jack is taking such good care of me."

And Emma had no one.

She'd come to town almost a year ago, to be the new librarian. Because she was shy, it had taken her a little while to make friends, but everyone liked her. Ryan had discovered her by accident, while doing the shopping for Billy, his housekeeper, after he'd sprained his ankle.

The instant attraction surprised Ryan, even repulsed him, but Emma wasn't a lady who expected attention. She offered her help when the food he'd piled up began to slip. Then she'd continued, pushing her almost-empty buggy away.

After having everyone trying to push him into some woman's arms, any woman's arms, Emma's disinterest was...enticing. He found himself asking about her. Then he'd actually gone into the new library for the first time on some ridiculous excuse.

Again she'd helped him, suggesting a book for Billy to read, when Ryan knew Billy would think he'd lost his mind. And then she'd walked away.

No interest at all.

No flirting, no pushiness, no war paint or suggestive clothes.

He'd stepped up to the counter to check the book out, and on impulse, he'd asked her to eat with him before he went home. He'd told her he hated to eat alone.

He'd struck a chord. She agreed eating alone was difficult and joined him. Her eyes, hazel, fringed with dark lashes, had brightened, her soft lips had stretched into a smile, and he'd wondered if she'd fooled him. She looked too good to be alone.

Had it been a carefully set trap?

But, over dinner, he'd realized her loneliness wasn't a trick. She never acted like he wanted anything but a dining companion.

And that's all he was, he'd assured himself. Just because he wanted to slide his fingers through her silky, dark hair. And touch her soft skin. No, all he wanted was a dining companion. Dropping by the library just at closing had become a habit, though. Dinner with Emma had become something he looked forward to. Then he'd gone home with her.

To talk.

And had spent the night.

He hadn't gone back to the library for three weeks. He'd felt too guilty to show his face. She wasn't a virgin, thank God. He felt enough guilt without that. But she hadn't been experienced, either.

And when he went back to the library, she'd never said a word about his absence.

Just as she hadn't said a word about the baby.

"Ryan? Are you all right?" Beth asked, bringing him back to the present.

"Yeah, I'm fine. I'll go now. I have someone else to visit."

"Who?" Jack asked, a frown on his face. "I hadn't heard of any friends—"

"No one you know!" Ryan exclaimed, backing to the door. He wasn't sure what he was going to do, but he wasn't ready to tell his family what had happened. He waved and hurried out of the room.

* * *

Emma felt the tears seeping from her closed eyes, getting sopped up by her hair. She didn't know why she was crying. It must be because she was so weak. And frightened about the future.

"You knew he would be upset," she muttered to herself. Especially to find out from someone else. Maybe one of the nurses had told him. After all, she'd put his name on the birth certificate.

That had been a mistake.

But she'd intended to tell him about the baby. Only she'd been so tired, so sick, she hadn't had the strength to deal with him.

And she'd been desperately afraid he'd insist on an abortion.

There was no way she'd agree to such a thing. She'd been left on a doorstep when she'd been born. At first, she'd been sick, so no one had wanted to adopt her. The years slipped away, and she moved from one foster home to another. She got healthier, but she'd never been the "cute" baby anyone wanted.

She'd vowed that her baby, if she ever had one, would be loved, wanted. And that was a vow she'd keep, no matter what. She had to be back at work next Monday, but she'd prepared a little space for her baby behind the counter. She'd take Andrea with her.

So far, however, she couldn't even get out of bed without assistance. She hoped and prayed she got better fast. Because she couldn't afford too much time in the hospital. And she couldn't stay in bed at home. It was going to take her forever to pay the hospital bill as it was.

Her door opened again, and the man she loved, the man who hated her, came back into the room. At least he wasn't yelling this time. But she reached for the call button anyway. She was too weak to deal with him now.

"Emma, are you all right?"

His softly worded question took her by surprise. But she knew better than to read anything into it. The nurse had probably warned him not to be so noisy.

"I'm fine. I'm sorry someone told you—"

"They didn't. I was looking at—at the babies when they brought yours in. With the card listing me as the father."

Yours. He couldn't have chosen a better way to make it clear he had no interest in the baby. "I'm sorry," she whispered and looked toward the small window.

The door opened again. "Ryan Nix, I told you not to come in here again." Margie Long, the nurse who'd thrown him out last time, glared at him.

"Come on, Mrs. Long, I'm being civilized. I just wanted to ask a few questions," he protested, glaring at Emma because he'd probably figured she'd summoned the nurse.

"Emma, dear, do you want visitors?"

Emma kept staring toward the window, knowing if she looked at Ryan, she wouldn't be able to send him away. "No, I'm tired."

"Emma!" Ryan protested, but she continued to stare at that tiny window, using it as a lifeline to get her through his visit.

"Sorry, Ryan, but new mothers are the bosses around here. Out you go." She took him by the arm and tugged him out.

Emma didn't move until she heard the door close. Then she stared where Ryan had been, wishing she'd had the strength to stare at him. To memorize those features, to remember his gentle touch. His loving.

She'd believed his touch had been loving. Instead, it had just been sexy. She didn't know a lot about men, hadn't believed they could make love and feel nothing.

Now she knew. Ryan had made it very clear.

So it was just her and baby Andrea. She'd prepared in every way she could so they wouldn't need help. But she hadn't planned on being so weak. Still, they'd make it, the two of them.

She was determined.

"Didn't you read that birth card?" Ryan demanded, angry again. "She says I'm the father. Doesn't that give me some rights?"

"Sure does, if you're also the husband. Otherwise, nope. Have you told your mother?" she asked, a scolding tone in her voice that irritated him even more. He didn't need her to tell him his mother would be upset with him.

"No. Damn it, I just found out a few minutes ago!"

"Oh." The woman pressed her lips together. "We were all a little surprised ourselves."

He thought about all the trips to the doctor Beth

had had. "Didn't she have prenatal care?" his voice rising in concern and anger.

"She said she did, in Buffalo." There was doubt in Mrs. Long's voice. Buffalo, Wyoming, wasn't large, but it did have a bigger hospital than Franklin, their town.

"Buffalo? Why there?"

"I guess she didn't want anyone here to know. There were a few whispers, but she wasn't dating anyone, so we all thought she'd just gained weight. She wore loose clothing." After another pause, she added, "You two broke up a long time ago, didn't you?"

"Yeah."

"Maybe she started seeing someone else, but she put your name on the certificate."

Fierce protectiveness wouldn't allow him to let even the whisper of such a tale get started. "No! No, the baby's mine."

"Okay."

"What's wrong with her? I know you said it's because she just gave birth, but I saw Beth, and she's doing fine."

"Miss Davenport had complications."

"Is the baby okay? She seems small."

"Oh, she's a fine little darling, as sweet as can be," Mrs. Long said, a grandmotherly smile on her face.

"Then why is Emma so pale?"

They'd reached the nurse's desk. "She's normally pale, I believe," Mrs. Long said.

"Don't give me that," Ryan snarled. "I want to know what's wrong."

"You're not her husband, Ryan. You don't have the right to know her health status."

"Is Steve her doctor? Did he deliver the baby?" he asked, naming an old friend, the man who'd delivered his son, the man who'd tried to save both Merilee and his child after the accident.

The elevator opened and another nurse arrived at the desk. "Sorry I'm late, Margie. Hi, Ryan. You here to see Beth's baby? I heard she delivered today."

"Yeah, Susan. I've seen him. He's a fine boy."

She reached over and patted his arm. "Good for you. I knew you'd come through, even if it is tough."

He and Susan had gone to school together. If Margie Long was going off duty, he knew he'd have a better chance getting information from Susan. Maybe he could even visit Emma again.

"Don't let this young man near room 212. She doesn't want any visitors," Margie said, as she bent down to get her purse. "Besides, she's not well enough for them."

Then she nodded to Ryan and left.

"Who's in 212?" Susan asked.

Ryan answered, since Margie had left. "Emma Davenport."

"Are you and Emma together again, after all this time? I thought—"

"No. But she had my baby today and Mrs. Long wouldn't tell me anything."

Susan was stunned by his blunt statement. "Your baby?" she asked, her voice rising.

"Yes. And I want to see Emma."

"I can't let you in that room. Not after Margie said not to. I'd get fired." Susan looked over her shoulder, as if she feared Margie might be hiding around the corner.

Ryan sighed in frustration. "Okay, can you tell me why she looks like death warmed over?"

Susan pulled out the chart and scanned it quickly. "I'm not supposed to, but I could, uh, generally tell you a few things."

Chapter Two

There hadn't been much in Emma's file because she hadn't had any prenatal care records there. Steve had written a note that he'd requested information from the Buffalo facility.

Emma had reported to the nurses that she'd had gestational diabetes and high blood pressure. Plus, she'd bled too much during delivery and had had to receive a blood transfusion, which had further weakened her.

Susan couldn't tell him anything else.

Since she again refused his request to see Emma a third time, he gave up and left the hospital—after one more peep at the tiny baby wrapped in pink.

Ryan stood on the hospital steps, staring at the town he'd lived near all his life. But suddenly, everything had changed. What was he going to do?

He couldn't accept what had happened. He couldn't pretend to be a happy new father...or an anxious husband. He doubted he would survive risking his heart again. Laced with his mourning for his wife and child had been utter guilt. Though he hadn't committed a traffic violation, he'd walked away from the accident that killed them.

Many nights he'd crawled into bed wishing he wouldn't wake up the next morning. That first night he'd slept with Emma had been the only time he'd arisen with satisfaction in his heart, contentment. Then the guilt had tripled. How could he enjoy life again when Merilee and Ryan, Jr. were lost to the world? Creature comforts shouldn't be a part of his life. He'd chastised himself for three weeks.

Then he'd gone back to the library, unable to stay away, telling himself he and Emma would return to their old relationship, having dinner together. If, that is, she'd even speak to him.

She'd welcomed him as a friend. No questions, no complaints, no expectations. He was amazed. When he'd kissed her again, she'd opened to him. He hadn't been able to resist.

For two months they'd made love on a regular basis. Each time he'd provided protection, having no intention of creating a child. No intention of a future. He'd condemned himself each time he thought about his behavior. So, he tried not to think, burying his conscience beneath the surface.

Until Emma had talked of a future, a family. Like a sore that had been festering beneath the skin, his conscience had erupted like a volcano, hurting Emma.

She'd already been pregnant.

That thought tore at him each time it came.

So, he still couldn't contemplate a future. But he could provide for Emma and the baby. He spun on his heels and reentered the hospital, heading straight for the business office.

"Oh, hi, Ryan, can I help you?" a friend of Merilee's asked. Damn, that was the problem with small towns. You couldn't swing a cat without hitting someone you knew.

"Yeah. I need to settle Emma Davenport's bill."

The woman stared at him. "Why?" His face must've reflected his feelings about being questioned. She hurriedly added, "We don't reveal financial information about patients unless it's family or they've okayed it."

"I'm the father of her child. I provide for—I'm paying the bill."

"Oh!" the woman exclaimed and got busy pulling Emma's record. She gave him the total amount due so far and offered a payment plan.

Ryan pulled out a checkbook. "No. I'll settle with you now. If there are other charges, please send them to me. You have my address, don't you?"

"Yes, of course."

He pressed his lips tightly together before adding, "Anything she wants, make sure she gets it."

She nodded, still staring at him.

He didn't wait around to see if she had more questions. Instead, he hurried to his truck. After driving the short distance to Dr. Steve Lambert's office, he strode in and asked to see the doctor.

"Mercy, Ryan, you sick?" the receptionist asked.

"No, Mrs. McCallister. I want to ask him some questions. Oh, and I need to pay Emma Davenport's bill."

He got the same reaction from her as he'd had at the hospital. He knew the town would be rocking with gossip about him by evening.

"Uh, Miss Davenport worked out a payment plan," Mrs. McCallister said. "She's already made one payment since she arranged for the doctor to make the delivery."

"When did she make the arrangements? I understood she was seeing a doctor in Buffalo."

"She came in two weeks ago."

Her response made Ryan even more anxious to talk to the doctor. "Give me the total she owes," he ordered tersely, "plus the cost for today." He already had his checkbook in hand.

When he'd taken care of that, he sat down in a chair in the waiting room, moodily watching the other patients. Several women were there with small children, and it didn't take much of an effort to see Emma visiting the office in the future.

Emma and the baby. He didn't even know the child's name. But he felt sure Emma had picked one out. She seemed to have prepared for the baby's arrival in every other way.

A few moments later, the receptionist called his name. "The doctor will see you now."

Ryan was led into his friend's office.

Steve stood as he entered and offered his hand. "Hey, pal. Long time no see. What's up?"

"I want to talk to you about Emma Davenport."

Steve's head snapped up and he stared at Ryan. "Why?"

"Because that's my child you delivered earlier today."

Steve's expression didn't change. "I wondered."

"I didn't know until I got to the hospital to see Beth. They brought the baby in with its birth-record card while I was looking at Beth's little boy." Ryan wanted Steve to understand that he wouldn't have abandoned Emma as he had if he'd known.

"Sorry you found out that way. When she first came in, two weeks ago, I asked about the father, but she refused to say anything."

Ryan wasn't surprised. In fact, the surprising thing was that she'd put his name on the certificate. But he suddenly remembered her talking about being a throwaway baby, a child no one had wanted. No birth certificate, no parents. He realized Emma wouldn't do that to her child, even if it would've been easier for her.

"Why didn't she come to you earlier?"

Steve shrugged. "I suppose to hide her pregnancy."

"Did she really do prenatal care in Buffalo?"

Steve didn't move, didn't reach for a file. "You know I'm legally not supposed to tell you about her medical history, don't you, Ryan?"

"Damn it, I'm the one responsible for her being in the hospital, Steve! I have a right to know."

"The last I heard, it takes two people to create a baby."

Ryan leaped to his feet and strode across the small

office and back again. "Just tell me what I need to do. Her face has no color at all, and she looks so sad. Are they both all right?"

"The baby is fine."

Ryan's heart twisted in pain. "And Emma?"

With a sigh, Steve reached for a file on his desk. "I just got the information faxed from Buffalo. She had gestational diabetes and high blood pressure. The labor was long and hard. Too much bleeding," he added, a frown on his face. "We had to give her a transfusion."

"But she'll be all right?"

Steve continued looking at the chart. Then he looked at Ryan. "They told her to quit work at six months. She was working until an hour before she delivered."

"Why? Why would she do that? Didn't she care about her baby?" Ryan knew that didn't make sense. Emma wasn't like that.

"I would guess she worked because she needed her job to support herself and the baby."

"I would've—!" Ryan protested. But he broke off. She hadn't even told him about the baby, much less asked for his help. And he couldn't blame her. His behavior seven months ago hadn't offered friendship, let alone marriage. "But you said she'll be all right?"

"If she gives herself time to recuperate. She'll probably need some help the first week or two at least. I'd like her to not go back to work for six weeks. But I suspect she'll refuse my advice."

"You haven't told her yet?"

"I haven't talked to her since the delivery. I'll check in with her before I go home this evening."

It was already half past four. Ryan knew Steve was a dedicated doctor, beloved by everyone in town for his selfless efforts on their behalf.

"I'll hire someone to take care of her," he said. "She won't be left alone."

"Good."

He stood. "She'll be released from the hospital in a couple of days?"

"I'll try to keep her there that long. She told me two weeks ago she wouldn't be staying more than one night."

"But she didn't know then how hard a time she'd have, right?" Ryan, after having seen Emma, wasn't sure she would even be able to walk in a week's time, much less care for a newborn.

Steve's closed expression, as if he didn't want to discuss anything else, was his only answer. "Look, let me know when she's getting out and I'll be there to get her settled in."

"Ryan, someone checking on her every day won't be enough. She's weak and determined to nurse her child. If she accomplishes that, it will be a miracle. Forget cleaning, cooking, bathing the baby. And she'll need more. She'll need companionship. I'm seriously worried about her because she seems so alone...so sad."

Guilt again built in Ryan's chest. Okay, so he'd paid a few bills. He had the money. It wasn't much of a sacrifice. But Emma's sad eyes popped into his head, alongside Beth's look of joy.

Ryan paced the doctor's office again, facing a difficult decision. The guilt won out.

"Okay, I'll take her back to the ranch with me. Billy can do the cooking and cleaning. And I'll hire one of the cowboys' wives to stay with her every day until she's better. Will that do?"

The doctor's compassionate gaze settled on Ryan's face. "If that's the best you can do, I guess so. It's better than her being on her own."

Ryan didn't put much effort into his goodbyes. He wanted away from that look. Away from what he was facing. And he had a lot to do.

Once he reached his truck, he took out his cell phone and called the ranch.

"Billy, drop everything and get ready for two guests."

"Hi, boss. Your mom and dad coming to see the new grandbaby?"

"Yeah, but they're staying at Beth's. Uh, Emma Davenport and her baby are going to recuperate at the ranch."

Silence followed his announcement. Then Billy said, "Okay. How old is the baby?"

Emma had visited the ranch a few times and had quickly become a favorite with Billy. Her quiet appreciation for his efforts, plus her offers to help, had pleased him.

"Her baby was born today. Give Emma the downstairs bedroom and clean out the little room across the hall. I'll bring home some baby stuff to go in there. Get help if you need it."

Ryan didn't give himself time to think. He hurried

to the one department store in town to get whatever he'd need to accommodate the baby. Later, if Emma didn't want any of it, he could give it to Beth, or keep it for when she, Jack and his namesake visited.

The saleswoman, another hometown friend, eagerly sold him everything ever known to mankind made for a baby. Memory of Emma's sad eyes had him buying the most gaily-colored items offered. He helped load everything in the back of his truck, ready to head for home.

His stomach growled and he considered stopping for a bite to eat, but that made his thoughts immediately fly to Emma and their dinners. It wasn't the first time this had happened. In fact, he'd refused to come into town in the afternoons for the past few months.

He slammed into the cab of his truck and drove faster than he should have to reach the safety of the ranch. Soon even the ranch wouldn't be safe.

Emma and the baby would be there.

Emma was encouraged by the slight increase of strength she felt the next morning. She almost had to crawl to the bathroom in her room, but she made it without calling for help.

The nurse came in just as she left the bathroom and helped her back to bed. Emma couldn't refuse since she was trembling all over.

"You should've called for help," the nurse chided. "Doctor said you weren't to get out of bed."

"I have to get stronger so I can go home today," Emma said, trying to smile at the woman.

"Lawsy-mercy, after the time you had? Doctor won't even think of letting you leave today. You could stay in bed for a week and it would still be too early."

Panic built in Emma, but she tried to hide it. "I don't need that long. Besides, I can't afford it, you know. Babies are expensive."

The nurse gave her a kindly smile. "Oh, you don't have to worry about that. Ryan took care of everything."

Thank goodness she was already in the bed, or she would've collapsed on the floor. "What did you say?" she demanded, but her voice was faint.

"Uh, I shouldn't have—I thought it would reassure you. I'm sorry." The nurse began backing toward the door. "I'll bring your breakfast."

As soon as she was alone, Emma reached for the phone beside her bed. When the billing office answered, she demanded to know her balance.

"Your balance is zero, Miss Davenport," the woman said cheerfully.

"How can that be? I haven't paid anything."

"Oh, your baby's father paid everything. We're supposed to bill him if there are any other charges. So, you have nothing to worry about."

Emma hung up the phone without answering. Nothing to worry about. She had put Ryan's name on the birth certificate because she knew how much that meant to a child later in life. She hadn't known either her father or her mother's name. Her child would know.

But she hadn't done it so Ryan would feel forced

to pay for the baby…and her. She'd always known he was a good man. And she'd found out about his wife and son afterwards. As much as his words had hurt her, stunned her, she'd understood.

She should've carried out her plan to have the baby in Buffalo, but it was an hour's drive away, and she'd got frightened that she wouldn't be able to make the drive by herself.

Seven months ago, she'd even considered giving up the job she loved and moving away then, while she could still have managed. But she hadn't, because she'd harbored a foolish hope that Ryan would change his mind. That he'd walk back through the doors of the library and ask her out to dinner again.

Foolish, foolish Emma.

With tears in her eyes, she pushed up from the pillow and surveyed her room. Her suitcase was on the floor by the window, still packed, though standing open. Last night the nurse had helped her don her own nightgown. While not fancy, at least it didn't have gaps down the back, like the hospital gown she had worn.

So, all she'd have to do was make her way to the chair beside her suitcase, get dressed, toss in her nightgown, and leave. Stopping to collect Andrea on the way, of course.

The thought of walking to her car alone was enough to exhaust her. Carrying a suitcase and her baby seemed an impossibility. But she didn't want Ryan paying any more.

He didn't want them, either of them.

As she was contemplating what she had to do, the

door opened and the nurse entered with a breakfast tray. She raised the head of the bed, then put the tray on the bed table and slid it in front of Emma.

"You'll feel stronger once you eat your breakfast," she advised cheerfully. "And Doctor will be in soon to visit with you. He came last night, but you were already asleep and he didn't want to wake you."

"Oh, I'm sorry," she whispered. She barely remembered him from the delivery, but she'd liked him when she'd visited him two weeks ago to ask him to deliver her baby.

"No problem. He thought you getting some rest was more important than him poking around on you. Actually, you're doing much better than any of us expected. You were in labor a long time. Why, Beth Kirby came in after you and delivered a couple of hours before you did."

"Beth's here? She had her baby?" Emma asked, joy on her face. She'd loved Beth almost as much as Ryan, feeling she'd finally found a sister. "Are she and the baby all right? What did she have?"

"Mercy, if I'd known that information would've cheered you up, I'd have told you at once," the nurse said.

Emma blushed, embarrassed by letting her emotions show. She hoped the nurse didn't tell Beth she'd been so eager for news. It would shock Ryan's sister after Emma had rejected her offer of continuing friendship.

"I—I know her."

"Well, of course you do. She's your baby's aunt.

She had a little boy, and both are doing just fine. You've never seen a prouder daddy than Jack Kirby. He hasn't left the hospital since they came in except to buy the biggest bouquet of roses in town. These daddies, you know how they..." She broke off abruptly, a stricken look on her face.

Emma knew what had caused her to grow silent. There were no flowers in her room. More importantly, there was no proud father watching his daughter through the nursery window, hovering over the mother's bed.

"I'm so sorry, I—"

"Don't worry about it, please. When will you bring my baby to me?"

"After you see the doctor."

Emma nodded, but she was anxious to hold her baby again. "Then I'd better get started on my breakfast."

The nurse, still embarrassed, tried to respond in a normal voice. As soon as she made sure Emma had everything she needed, she hurried from the room.

Ryan stood at the nursery window, staring at the pink bundle. The baby hadn't moved or shown any sign of life since he'd arrived. When a nurse entered the nursery, he rapped on the window and pointed to the baby girl.

The nurse smiled and moved the baby to the front row of the window. Wouldn't she have noticed if something was wrong? Ryan wanted to be reassured that the baby was breathing.

Just as he decided to knock on the window again,

one little baby fist, clenched, moved to the rosebud mouth and the baby made some sucking motions.

Maybe she *was* kin to him. Dinnertime had always been high on his list. A small smile slipped across his lips, until he heard footsteps in the hallway.

Steve Lambert joined him. "Little miracles, aren't they?"

"Uh, yeah. I don't see Beth's baby."

"He's probably in the room having breakfast with his mom."

"Isn't Emma—I mean, it—the baby seems hungry."

"Emma indicated she wanted to breast-feed, but I had them give the baby sugar water until this morning. Emma will probably try today."

"What did she say when you told her last night she was going to the ranch with me?" That question had filled his mind even as he and Billy set up the nursery last night. He didn't think she'd easily agree.

"I didn't talk to her. She was already asleep when I got to her room last night."

"You were here that late? What happened?"

"An emergency. Barney Landers cut himself and had to have stitches. I got to Emma's room by seven-thirty. But she'd already had her dinner and gone to sleep. I decided not to wake her. The nurses said she was doing all right. She needed the rest."

"Are you going to see her now?"

"Yeah. Want to join me? We'll face her together."

Ryan would've liked to say no. He thought she'd agree with the doctor more easily than she would with him there. But it felt cowardly to hide behind his friend. "Sure," he agreed and walked down the hall with Steve.

He dreaded every step that brought him closer to Emma.

Chapter Three

Emma gathered her strength and shoved back the blanket and sheet covering her. If she kept putting it off, she would never get out of the hospital.

And she'd decided it would be better to leave before the doctor got there...if she could manage it.

The door opened and she snatched the cover back to her chin.

Dr. Lambert caught the movement. "You need some assistance to get to the facilities? I'll call a nurse," he said gently and picked up her call button.

"No, I—" she began, but she stopped as Ryan came into view.

"Yes, Doctor?" the nurse called from behind Ryan's wide shoulders.

"I think Miss Davenport needs some assistance, nurse. We'll wait outside the room until she's ready." The doctor turned and pushed Ryan ahead of him, closing the door.

"What is it, dear? Are you feeling sick?"

"No, I was getting up to dress and—"

"You were what? You'll do no such thing. I told you you were to stay in bed. Well, I never!" She tucked the covers tightly around Emma, and before Emma could ask her not to mention her indiscretion, she opened the door and announced to the doctor that Miss Davenport was getting out of bed to dress. "I'll willingly help her, sir, if that's what you want, but the last instructions I received were for her to stay in bed."

"Thank you, nurse," he replied. "Let me visit with the patient, and then I'll get back to you."

"Yes, sir."

Emma lay back against the pillow, figuring she'd blown it. She'd probably receive a lecture with Ryan watching. She closed her eyes and kept them closed, even when she heard the heavy footsteps.

"Miss Davenport?"

She opened her eyes, but she turned her head away, staring at that small window again. "Yes?"

"I gather you're anxious to leave us."

Her teeth sank into her bottom lip. Then she said, "I'm not complaining about the service, Doctor, but my baby and I are ready to go home."

He moved to stand beside her, taking her hand in his. "I think you'd both be better off if you wait a couple of days."

Emma took a quick glance at Ryan's chiseled features and then looked at the doctor. "I—I really can't afford that. I promise I'll be careful. My baby will be—"

"You can't go, Emma," Ryan announced, as if it were his decision.

She refused to look at him.

"Doctor, I'll follow your directions, I promise, but—"

"My directions are to stay in the hospital," the man said gently, looking at her.

"I paid your bills, Emma," Ryan announced.

She was glad she already knew he'd done so. "I'll pay you back," she said, still avoiding looking at him.

"Emma, you and your baby are my responsibility."

"No!" she exclaimed, glaring at him. "I and *my* baby have nothing to do with you!"

"The hell you don't! Why am I listed as the father if that's true?"

"Ryan, wait outside."

Emma stared at the doctor, grateful for his intervention.

"Steve, I need to—" Ryan protested.

"Ryan, wait outside." His voice was a little more insistent, and he stared at Ryan.

Emma closed her eyes. She heard Ryan's footsteps leaving the room.

"Tell him I'll have his name removed. I didn't mean—"

"Are you telling me he's not the father of your baby?" the doctor asked calmly.

Her eyes snapped open and she stared at him. Then she closed them again.

"That's right," she whispered. "I lied."

"You're lying now, Emma, and we both know it."

Emma opened her eyes again and stared at the doctor. "I didn't want my baby to have to wonder who her parents were. I didn't intend to make Ryan pay for what he didn't want. That's why I need to go home today."

"How will going home today change anything?"

She tried to sit up and he raised the head of the bed for her. "I see you know him. I know him, too. He's a good man, but he didn't want—want me or the baby. I don't want him paying out of guilt. I'll manage. I promise I'll hold to the payment plan. Please don't let him pay you."

"Too late, Emma. He's already paid," the doctor said with a grin. "Hey, it's not a problem for him."

With the tears she could no longer hold back, she muttered, "It's a problem for me."

He pulled up a chair and sat down, shaking his head. "We've got something more important to talk about."

The seriousness of his tone immediately frightened her. "Is Andrea okay? The nurse said—they haven't brought her in. No! No, she isn't— No!"

The door swung open and Ryan rushed in. "What is it? What's wrong?"

The doctor ignored him and stood again, putting his hands on Emma's shoulders. "Emma, your baby is fine. That's not what I meant. She's fine. The nurse is going to bring her in in a few minutes to show you how to nurse her."

"You told her something was wrong with the

baby?'' Ryan demanded, his voice rising in alarm. ''But you said she was fine.''

''You people are crazy,'' the doctor said with a smile. ''Listen to me. The baby—what's-her-name—is perfectly healthy.''

''Andrea Leigh,'' Emma said, wiping her cheeks, subsiding since the doctor wasn't alarmed. She felt ridiculous for making such a fuss.

''Leigh?'' Ryan repeated, disbelief in his voice. ''You named her after my mother?''

She heard the anger rising in his voice. She drew a deep breath. ''Yes, Andrea Leigh.''

''Hoping to get my mother on your side?''

''Ryan…'' the doctor said in warning.

Emma had regained control, however. She looked at Ryan, really looked at him for the first time, and said, ''Yes, I named her after her grandmother. Because she's the only grandmother Andy will ever have.''

Then she turned away from Ryan. ''What did we need to discuss, Doctor?''

Ryan stared at Emma. Two minutes ago, she was almost hysterical. Then she'd stared him down when he asked about the baby's name.

His mother was going to be upset enough about the situation without discovering the baby was her namesake.

One more problem to deal with.

''No!'' Emma shouted, upset again.

Ryan came back to the present to stare at her. ''What's going on?''

Steve sighed. "I explained about your offer to take Emma and the baby home with you while she recovered."

She turned a stubborn look toward him. "No, thank you."

Politeness with an attitude.

"Steve said you can't go home, Emma. You need someone to take care of you." She'd be reasonable. After all, he was a responsible man.

"No."

No attitude now. Just an emotionless firm answer.

"Emma," the doctor said, intervening again, "If you want to leave the hospital, you have to have someone to help you with the baby, to clean and cook for you. Do you have anyone who can do that?"

Emma stared straight ahead, ignoring both men. "I'll manage."

"Emma, I don't want to have to ask Social Services to step in."

Emma gasped, her hand going to her throat.

"Steve," Ryan protested, knowing how much that threat would hurt Emma.

Steve held up his hand. "I don't want to, but I'm not going to let you risk your baby's health, Emma. Or your own. I don't want you to lift anything, even your baby, for at least a week."

It upset Ryan when Emma's cheeks whitened. "Emma, Billy's planning on you coming. He'll take care of everything, and I'll hire one of the wives on the ranch to help you every day. You won't have to worry about me bothering you."

He'd thought his words would help, but she looked even more devastated. Frowning, he tried to think about what he'd said to upset her, but he couldn't figure out what it was.

"It's the only way, Emma, if I'm going to let you out of here before at least a week is up," Steve added.

"Please, couldn't I—"

"No."

Ryan wanted to rail at her. She made his offer sound like torture. He was trying to help. What was wrong with her? But he didn't need Steve's glare to warn him to keep quiet. Every time he spoke it only made matters worse.

"If I agree to go to the ranch, can Andy and I go today?" Emma asked, her voice trembling.

Steve reached out and covered her hand resting on the blanket. "No, but you can go after I see you in the morning."

Ryan held his breath, waiting for her answer. It was because it was the only safe thing to do, of course. His tension had nothing to do with Emma...or her baby.

With her lashes lowered, she said, slowly, "All right."

"Good, I'm glad. Now I won't have to worry about that beautiful little girl," Steve said, patting her hand again.

Ryan watched that hand, fighting the urge to tell him to take his hands off Emma. Which was ridiculous. Steve wasn't that kind of man. Emma was safe with him.

Then Emma turned her gaze on him. "Can Billy take me to the apartment first? I'll need—"

"We have everything you need. He set up a nursery last night." That wasn't quite honest. Billy hadn't done it by himself, but Emma didn't seem to want Ryan involved in anything connected to her or her baby.

Not that he blamed her. Ever since he'd seen that tiny baby, with him named as the father, and realized Emma had already been pregnant when he'd shut her out of his life, guilt had filled him.

Damn it, he'd been right, believing he shouldn't have anything to do with family. His mistake was not explaining that to Emma *before* he—

"Ryan?" Steve called, interrupting his self-castigation. "I think Emma will be able to leave about ten in the morning. Is that all right with you?"

"Yes, of course."

Emma said nothing, staring out the small window. The door opened again behind Ryan and he automatically turned to see who had arrived.

The nurse had stepped into the room. But she wasn't alone. That pink bundle was in her arms. He stepped closer, wanting a better view of the baby. But then he looked at Emma. The panic-stricken look on her face stopped him.

Did she think he would hurt the child? She considered him a monster? He might not have chosen to have another child, but he wouldn't harm the baby.

His features stiff, he stepped away from the new arrivals and noted the relief on Emma's face. The message was clear. She was coming to his ranch because she had no choice, but she wanted nothing to do with him. Nor did she want him to touch her child.

Steve was standing beside Emma and reached out to pat her shoulder. "The nurse is going to help you start nursing your little girl, but they're not going to bring the baby to you tonight. The nurses will give her more sugar water. I want you to have one more night of sleep before you leave."

"Oh, but I can—"

"Not tonight," he said firmly but cheerfully. "We'll leave you alone now for your lesson. Goodbye, Emma."

Ryan didn't know whether to add his goodbye or not. Maybe it would be best if he just faded from view.

When he and Steve reached the hallway, he walked beside his friend, saying nothing.

"You know," Steve finally said, "I'm disappointed in you, Ryan."

Ryan's head snapped up and he stared at his friend. "What? Why?"

"I thought you'd make a little more effort to support Emma. I think the past few months have been difficult for her."

"You think I don't know that?" Ryan demanded, his voice hoarse. "Do you think I haven't condemned myself over and over again for the way I treated her? But she doesn't want anything from me. She hardly speaks to me, avoids looking at me. If she had anyone else to turn to, she wouldn't be coming home with me. That much was clear."

Steve shook his head. "I'm not so sure. She could be afraid to get close to you again."

"Yeah, because she hates me." He started walking again. "I'm doing what I can. She'll be taken care of, and I'll keep my distance. That's the best I can do to help her out."

This time, Steve didn't argue with him.

After an almost sleepless night, Ryan arrived at the hospital a little early the next morning. He'd talked to Jack yesterday evening and knew Beth was going home today, too. Jack had arranged for a temporary housekeeper to help Beth during the day when he returned to work as the only local attorney.

Ryan knocked on Beth's door.

"Come in," Jack called.

"Everyone packed?" Ryan asked, trying to keep his voice cheerful.

"Come in, Ryan," Beth called, smiling. "Yes, we're packed. We're just waiting for Steve to okay everything."

"Good. So you and junior are doing okay?"

"Yes, fine. Better than you, I'd say." Beth looked at her husband before shifting her gaze back to Ryan.

"Stayed up too late working," Ryan muttered.

"I see. I thought maybe you were worrying about not telling me about Emma."

Ryan glared at Jack, figuring he'd told his wife about Emma and the baby.

"I didn't say a word," Jack protested, rightly interpreting Ryan's glare.

"For heaven's sake, Ryan, the entire town is talking. I had to pretend I already knew when my visitors spilled the beans. Why didn't you tell me? How long have you known?''

"Beth, I—I found out when I saw the baby in the nursery. It's been a shock." What an understatement, Ryan thought. He still didn't know what he was going to do.

"Oh. Well, I want to go see her before I go home. She might not let me visit her if I don't.''

"Don't you need to wait for Steve?''

"I'll tell them at the nurse's desk where I am. Please?" Beth pleaded with her gaze as well as her words.

Ryan shrugged. "You'll get a better reception if you go without me.''

"But—but I heard you're taking her home to the ranch.''

Ryan stuck his hands in his jean pockets. "Yeah, but she hates my guts. She's going because she can't manage on her own. She didn't handle everything as well as you did.''

Beth stared at him before turning to her husband. "Go get a wheelchair. I want to take Jackson to show her.''

"You can't walk?" Ryan asked, worried.

"I can, but I worry about stumbling when I'm carrying the baby.''

Jack was quickly back with a wheelchair. While he was gone, Ryan had taken a closer look at his namesake. Ryan Jackson had weighed over eight pounds when he was born, and he hadn't lost much weight.

Emma's baby, on the other hand, had weighed only a little under six pounds. Ryan wouldn't have thought the difference in weight would matter, but it did.

Once Beth and Jackson were settled in the chair, with Jack pushing it, they all traveled the short distance to Emma's room. Ryan dreaded facing her today, but maybe she'd be nicer with Beth along. He knew Emma had liked Beth.

"Emma?" he called after rapping on the door.

"Yes?"

He pushed open the door. It was clear she hadn't recognized his voice. Shock was on her face.

"I'm not ready to go yet. I have to get dressed and—"

He gestured behind him. "I know. I brought you some visitors."

"Beth!" Emma called with joy when she saw his sister behind him.

"Emma, how are you? I heard you had a hard time. I didn't even know you were here until last evening," Beth explained as Jack wheeled her to Emma's bedside.

"Oh, you brought your little boy. Isn't he handsome! And so big. Andy's small," Emma said, beaming at her old friend.

"Andy? I thought you had a little girl."

"I did. Her name is Andrea." Emma shifted her gaze to Ryan quickly, then turned back to Beth.

Ryan couldn't help himself. "Andrea Leigh."

"You named her after Mom?" Beth asked, a big smile on her lips. "She'll be so pleased."

Emma glared at Ryan. "I didn't intend..."

The nurse entered with Emma's baby in her arms. "My goodness. I didn't know you had company, Miss Davenport. Do you want me to take your baby back to the nursery until the doctor gets here?"

"Oh, no. I'm ready for her. Did she have a good night?" Emma asked, her voice eager as she extended her arms.

"Oh, good," Beth exclaimed. "I'm dying to see her. You'll get to dress your baby in pretty clothes. Jack has already bought a pair of jeans for Jackson. Ugh!"

The two women examined both babies, rapidly exchanging compliments. Jack stood just behind Beth, glowing with pride. Ryan remained close to the door, trying to hide his desire to see the little girl.

His little girl.

He still found it hard to believe that, once again, he was a father. It was painful, because it made him think about Ryan, Jr., who would've been getting ready for kindergarten in the fall...if he hadn't died.

"Hey, Ryan," Jack called, "I bet you never thought a kid of yours would be so—so dainty. Are you afraid you'll break her when you hold her? I know I am when I hold Jackson and he's lots bigger."

His cheerful remark was followed by silence.

Ryan didn't know what to say. He'd never touched the child, much less held her.

Emma, however, didn't seem to have his problem. "Ryan hasn't held my child," she said quietly.

Beth patted Jack's hand as it rested on her shoulder. "It's not easy for Ryan, Emma. I know you've heard—give him time."

Emma held Andrea tightly against her. "I'm not making any demands on Ryan, Beth. I'll probably move after I'm able to take care of the two of us on my own. It will be better that way."

"Leave? Oh, no! No, Emma, don't leave," Beth protested.

Ryan was glad Beth had spoken. He was paralyzed with shock.

Then Beth, Jack and Emma all looked at him. Beth was the first to look away. Ryan knew what his sister and brother-in-law wanted. They wanted him to protest Emma's leaving, too.

But how could he?

He cleared his throat. "When is Steve supposed to be here?"

Jack said, "He told Beth she'd be able to leave around ten and it's a quarter to now."

"Good. I brought a car seat for—for Andrea."

That was the first time he'd called the baby by name. He took a quick look at Emma to see if she would protest his familiarity.

"Thank you," she whispered, not looking at him. "But I thought Billy was going to come."

"He's home fixing you a big lunch," Ryan said brusquely.

Another tense silence.

"Mom and Dad are going to be here in a couple of days," Beth said brightly. "They'll be so excited to know they have *two* grandchildren."

"I think it might be best if they don't know, since I'll be leaving soon, anyway." Another tense silence.

Then Emma spoke again. "I guess I'd better feed Andy now, before I get dressed."

As a hint for them to leave, Emma's words were blunt, but Beth didn't seem to take the hint. "Oh, you shouldn't dress, Emma. Just put on your robe. No one expects you to be the height of fashion, especially when you'll get back in bed as soon as you get to the ranch."

Emma raised her chin. "I don't have a robe, so I'll dress. But it won't take me long," she added with a quick look at Ryan, as if afraid he might get upset if she kept him waiting.

Ryan again felt guilt. Beth had received a new robe and gown from her parents to pack for her trip to the hospital. Emma had received no gifts.

"We'd better let you feed the baby," he said, sending a message to Beth that they should leave.

Emma nodded. "Thank you for coming to visit, Beth."

Beth reached out to touch her hand. "I've missed you, Emma. It won't be our last visit."

Then the three of them left Emma and baby Andrea alone.

Chapter Four

For the first time that morning, Emma was happy. Holding Andrea in her arms, nursing her, feeling so connected to another human, her baby, made a difference.

Even if Ryan rejected them, she had family. She had Andy. And her child wouldn't be hurt by Ryan's attitude as long as he kept his distance. She smoothed back the fuzzy dark hair that covered Andrea's head. Then she kissed her forehead.

The baby had learned her lesson about nursing quickly, and this morning seemed more eager, hungrier. Even the nurse had commented on it before she'd left the room.

The door opened and the nurse re-entered. "Still eating? She's got a good appetite for such a small one."

Emma beamed.

"Here," the nurse said, putting a large paper bag on the bed. "This is from Ryan."

Emma's happiness dissolved. "What is it?"

"One of those nice terrycloth robes they sell in the gift shop."

Humiliation surged through Emma. "I don't want it. Have him return it and get his money back."

The nurse looked shocked. She stepped closer to the bed. "Dear, you're being stubborn. You need to think about what's best for you. It will take too much energy to get dressed, just to undress again. Besides, let the man fuss over you. It'll make him feel good."

Emma almost burst into hysterical laughter. Fussing over her was the last thing Ryan wanted to do. It must've been Beth's idea to get her a robe. Emma realized it was her fault. She should've just said she preferred to dress.

Stiffly, she said, "Thank you."

Andrea shoved tiny fists against Emma's breasts and mewed in protest. She hurriedly helped the baby find the right spot again.

"Besides, if you don't stay relaxed, that sweet thing won't be able to eat well," the nurse added.

For the next couple of minutes both women stayed silent until Andrea fell asleep.

"Good job," the nurse said, reaching for the baby. "I'm going to lie her down here at the end of the bed so you can get up and slip into your new robe. Then I'll get the wheelchair. I left it out in the hall."

Emma did as the nurse instructed, standing to slide her arms into the soft robe. She'd never indulged in luxury, especially since she'd found out she was pregnant. She'd saved every penny for the future.

The nurse left her standing, holding on to the bed for support, and went out the door to fetch the wheelchair. When she reentered, she was accompanied by Ryan and Dr. Lambert.

It was the doctor and not Ryan who hurried to ease her into the wheelchair. "Good morning, Emma. I hear little Andrea took to nursing like a duck to water."

By the time Emma was seated in the chair, she was trembling again. Even if it was Beth's idea to get her the robe, she was grateful. "Yes, she's doing well." She nerved herself to look at Ryan. "Thank you for the robe."

He nodded, saying nothing.

Steve lifted her wrist to take her pulse. "I think you're doing better today, Emma, but I want you to take it easy. Let the others take care of both of you, okay? I'll be out in a few days to check on you."

"Thank you, Doctor." She suspected she was receiving such consideration because of Ryan. But the thought of dressing and coming to the doctor's office was more than she could consider at this moment.

"Are you all packed?" Dr. Lambert asked.

The nurse answered. "Yes, I've packed her bag for her."

Ryan, who still hadn't spoken, stepped forward and took the bag from the nurse.

"Well, then, off you go, Emma." The doctor picked up the baby and handed her to Emma. With baby Andrea in her arms again, Emma relaxed. No matter where they went, she and Andrea would manage.

Ryan watched Emma nestle the baby against her, her love obvious to all of them. She was going to be a wonderful mother. As Merilee had been. In fact, he'd complained that Merilee hadn't wanted him involved in Ryan, Jr.'s life until he got big enough to walk.

Emma didn't want him involved at all.

The baby suddenly opened her eyes, and Ryan would swear she was staring at him. Her eyes didn't have any particular color yet, but Ryan was entranced. It was the first time she'd been awake in his presence. It was all he could do to hold back an exclamation.

"Since you've got the bag, I'll push the wheelchair, Ryan," the nurse said.

"And I'll go release Beth and Jack. I know they're anxious to get home," Steve Lambert said. "See you in a few days." He left the room.

The nurse pushed Emma and the baby out of the room, and Emma could hear Ryan's boots as he followed. Almost like a family. Emma sharply reprimanded herself at such a thought. She had to keep herself from dreaming about a future with Ryan. It wasn't going to happen.

She had to remain strong.

Ryan stored Emma's suitcase in the back of his SUV, then he came back to the front of the car and opened the back-seat door by the baby carrier.

The nurse still stood behind the wheelchair and he realized she was waiting for him to pick up his child and put her in the carrier.

He drew a deep breath before bending toward Emma. He feared she wouldn't give up her child. But, after a hesitation, she let him take Andrea. Knowing her gaze was following his every move, he gently placed the baby in the seat and belted her in.

Andrea rubbed her tiny nose with her fists and stretched. Ryan watched in fascination, hoping she'd open her eyes again. Instead, she settled in and grew still, her eyes still closed.

"You did that well for a new daddy," the nurse said cheerfully. She hadn't lived in town all that long and had no idea Ryan had had another child. But he heard Emma gasp. She knew. He wondered how long after his outrageous behavior she had heard the story.

He cleared his throat. "Thanks." Then he looked at Emma, no expression on her face now. "Ready, Emma?"

She pushed with her arms to stand, but he'd already noted how weak she was. Without saying anything, he lifted her as easily as he had the baby and settled her in the front seat. Her gasp told him he'd surprised her, but then any consideration he offered her seemed to be a surprise.

He fastened the seat belt before she could move. Then he said his goodbye to the nurse. Emma, too, in a hoarse voice, thanked the nurse for her care.

With a smile, Ryan closed the door and rounded the vehicle to the driver's seat. "You okay?" he asked.

Emma nodded, but she said nothing.

The drive to the ranch was silent.

When he parked the car by the back porch, she undid her own seat belt.

"Don't move," he ordered. Then he took Andrea from the baby carrier and opened the front door on Emma's side to put the baby into her arms.

"Thank you," she murmured, never looking at him. Then she began sliding to the edge of the seat, as if she thought he would let her walk to the house.

Instead, he scooped her into his arms again, holding her against his chest. He refused to admit how good she felt there. But he'd missed her the past seven months.

Billy held the back door open, and Ryan carried Emma directly to the room they had prepared.

"The baby—Andrea's room is across the hall. I'll go put her in her bed." He looked over his shoulder to see Billy and Maria Carter, one of the wives who lived on the ranch, hovering in the doorway. "Maria will help you get into bed."

He could've asked Maria to take care of the baby, but one taste of holding her had left him hungering for more. He took the tiny infant from Emma—she surrendered the baby reluctantly—and headed for the newly established nursery.

Billy had remained by the door and reached out to pull back the blanket. "Aw, she's a beauty, Emma," he said, and Emma beamed.

Unwanted jealousy rose in Ryan. He wanted to please Emma, to bring that glorious smile to her face. But that wouldn't happen, he knew. She'd scarcely look at him, much less smile. And he couldn't blame her.

He carried Andrea into the nursery, but he didn't put her in the crib at once. He held her, taking his first good look at his child. She was perfectly formed, but he searched for signs of his parentage. Her hair was as dark as Emma's, while his was a soft brown. Her features were delicate, like her mother's. But as she opened her eyes again, he decided they would be blue, like his, instead of Emma's hazel eyes.

"Something wrong with the crib?" Billy asked behind him.

"No, but I haven't had a chance to look at her. Emma doesn't want me to touch her," he admitted.

"Is she yours?" Billy asked.

Ryan had expected the question from the moment he'd told Billy about the baby. But Billy had never asked, even when they'd worked on the nursery.

He turned, still holding the baby. "Yes, she's mine. But I didn't find out about her until I went to see Beth."

Billy nodded. "Better put her in the crib so she can rest. Little ones need a lot of sleep."

Reluctantly, Ryan lowered the baby into the crib.

"Put her on her back. That's what they recommend these days."

Ryan looked in surprise at the old cowboy. "How do you know that?"

"I started reading up on babies when Beth told us she was pregnant. Figured I'd need to baby-sit," Billy said with a grin. "Glad I did, 'cause now we got our own baby."

"Billy, Emma won't stay any longer than she has to. She's not happy about being here." Ryan figured he'd better warn Billy not to expect a future with little Andrea.

"Why not? You're the daddy. Where else would she and Emma be?"

Ryan didn't know, but he felt sure he'd find out.

But first, he'd spend some time with the baby he hadn't known about.

Emma heard Andy crying and stirred against her pillow. Her eyes were gritty from waking so frequently during the night. She'd thought she'd be much stronger after a week of Billy and Maria's good care.

And she *was* better. She could even rise by herself. She still wasn't carrying Andy. When Dr. Lambert had visited a couple of days ago, he'd warned her not to rush things.

But she had decided she was well enough. She'd stayed the recommended week. That was enough.

Her bedroom door opened and Maria tiptoed in, Andrea in her arms. "Are you awake? Someone wants an early breakfast."

"Of course," Emma agreed, shoving herself up to a sitting position. "What time is it?"

"It's six-thirty." Maria had been spending the night to be there when the baby awoke each night. Emma figured she must be as tired as Emma was.

Before she could comment, the door was pushed slightly open. "Everything all right?" Ryan called softly from the hallway.

Maria hurried back to the door after handing Emma the baby.

"Everything's fine. Andy woke up early," she whispered.

Emma listened intently. She'd only seen Ryan once in the week she'd occupied his home. She and Andy had been invisible to him. Occasionally she'd hear his voice in the evening as Billy served him dinner. Otherwise, he could've left the country as far as she was concerned.

And probably wanted to.

His indifference ate away at her comfort. She had never wanted to be a charity case again. Or to be unwanted. She'd promised herself Andy would never feel those emotions.

And that was why she was leaving today...if she could talk Maria into helping her.

Maria came back into the room after Emma had uncovered her breast and offered breakfast to her hungry child. Andy gulped down milk like she hadn't eaten in weeks.

"Oh, she's hungry, isn't she?" Maria asked with a laugh.

"She always is."

"Must take after her father," Maria said, her smile widening. "But she must have his metabolism, too. He eats like a horse but never gains weight."

Emma took a deep breath. She'd tried not to think about Ryan for any reason, but particularly in connection to Andy.

"Maria? Will you help me?"

As she had done all week, Maria immediately responded to Emma's question, scurrying to the bedside. ''Of course, Emma. What do you want me to do?''

''I want you to take us home.''

Maria's eyes widened in shock and she took a step back from the bed. ''What do you mean?''

''The doctor said I needed to stay here a week, and the week is up today. I'm ready to go home, but I can't drive myself. My car is in town.''

''But Ryan—does he know?''

''Of course he does.'' She wasn't lying. He'd been there when the doctor told her she had to stay a week. He'd be relieved when he came home to discover his tortuous generosity had ended.

''Well, of course, I can, but don't you think Ryan will want to—''

''No! You know he's putting in long hours. He'll be tired…and grateful to know he won't have to go out after his long hours in the saddle.'' Emma always knew when Ryan was in the house. There was a raw energy that filled the air, a sense that the day had ended when he came home.

''He *is* working long hours,'' Maria agreed, still frowning.

''I have everything ready at home, so you won't have to worry about me. And I imagine your husband is getting tired of you not being at home.'' She could tell she'd touched a sore spot by Maria's rueful look.

''He has complained, but he sure likes the extra money I'm earning.''

Emma swallowed her groan. She hated the thought of how much she owed Ryan. But she was stronger now. She could bring an end to his sacrifices by returning to her apartment.

Until she was well enough to move away.

"When do you want to go?"

"As soon as I feed her, I'll get dressed. While I'm doing that, if you could pack Andy's things...just the nightgowns Ryan provided, and a few of the disposable diapers." She'd bought cloth diapers, but those were at the apartment. Secretly, she hoped she could afford the disposable ones for a while. They certainly made life easier.

"Okay, I'll go start packing now. But you must eat breakfast before you go. Okay?"

Emma smiled. "I'd never turn down one of Billy's meals. That's a good idea."

Maria hurried from the room after Emma agreed.

In the kitchen Maria asked for Emma's breakfast....and decided to check with the old cowboy to see what he thought about Emma's plans.

"Billy, Emma needs her breakfast," she said as she entered, grateful there was no sign of her husband's employer.

"Early today, isn't she?" Billy asked, turning around from the sink.

Maria nodded, but she hurried on to more important things. "She says she's going home today."

Billy stared at her. "Today?"

"She said the doctor said she could go home after a week. It's been a week since she came. She said Ryan knows."

Bill stood there frowning. "You'd think he'd mention her going. But he don't talk about Emma. Or the baby. He sneaks in at night to look at Andy, but I don't think he's visited with Emma even once. I'd hoped—"

"Me, too. I guess that's why she wants to leave."

"Yeah," Billy agreed with a sigh. "Well, we can't hold her here, if that's what she wants."

"You don't think Mr. Nix will fire Tommy, do you?" Maria asked, worried for her husband's job.

"'Cause you did as Emma asked? You know better than that, Maria. The boss is fair."

Maria nodded. "I'll go start packing the baby's things. She wants to leave as soon as she's had breakfast."

"Okay, I'm going to pack her a basket of food to take with her. She shouldn't be on her feet much for a while yet."

About three o'clock, Ryan's cell phone rang. He pulled it out of his saddlebag, reining in his mount. "Hello?"

"Darling, can we come over this evening and see little Andrea?" his mother asked at once.

"Mom," he started, desperately looking for another reason to postpone their visit. His mother had called three nights ago, when they'd arrived from Florida, telling him Beth had said to call. That he had something to tell her.

He made a mental note to pay his sister back for her meddling. But in actuality, he was glad to confess before anyone else told his parents. However, he'd asked them not to visit for a few days, citing Emma's health.

"We're not going to ask her to run a marathon," Leigh Nix protested before Ryan could come up with anything. "But I want her to know we're excited about the baby."

With a sigh, he said, "Okay, Mom, but it'll have to be a short visit."

"Of course. Afterwards, we can talk."

Her words sounded ominous, but it wasn't anything he hadn't expected. "Sure."

After stowing the phone back in his saddlebag, he rode to the other side of the herd they were moving to talk to his manager. "Baxter, I'm going back to the house early. Everything okay?"

"We're doin' fine, boss. 'Bout time you took off early."

Ryan didn't bother acknowledging his manager's opinion. He couldn't tell the man the mother of his child didn't want him around. Everyone seemed to think Emma's living at the ranch was a permanent thing.

Maybe he did, too. He hadn't made any plans. He hadn't come to any decisions about the future, either. He'd drifted, staying away from the house until late, making sure he stayed out of Emma's way, getting a report from Billy each night.

But he'd snuck into Andrea's room before he went to bed each evening, unable to stay away from his beautiful child.

He guessed he was hoping that Emma, with good food and rest, would forget how much she hated him.

So far it hadn't worked.

He was about a half hour's ride from the house. After reaching home and caring for his horse, he strode to the house. Billy would be surprised to see him at this time of the day.

It would give his cook time to prepare something to serve when his parents came over. And he wanted to ready Emma for their visit.

"Something wrong, Boss?" Billy called as he stepped onto the porch.

"Nope," Ryan replied, taking the screen door from Billy's hands as they both moved into the kitchen. "But I can't stall Mom and Dad any longer. They're coming over tonight to see the baby. And Emma."

He didn't see Billy's face until after he'd gotten himself a drink of water. "What's wrong?" he asked, his heartbeat speeding up. "Is the baby sick? Emma?"

"They're not here," Billy replied.

Ryan turned to stone. Then his heart raced as he grabbed Billy's arm. "What do you mean? Emma's not well? Did she have to go to the doctor?"

"Nope. She told Maria she was only supposed to stay a week and asked her to take her to her apartment."

"Damn! When did she go?"

"This morning early, after breakfast."

Ryan didn't stop for any conversation. "Get her room ready. She's coming back."

Then he headed for his truck.

* * *

Emma had known going to her apartment would be tiring, both emotionally and physically. After all, she'd cut her connection to Ryan. No more fantasizing. She and Andrea were on their own.

She'd slept all day, waking only when Andrea had cried for her meals. And Emma had managed to eat some of the food Billy had thoughtfully sent home with her.

She'd just drifted off to sleep again when there was a loud banging on the door. Andrea, who was sleeping beside her mother to save Emma frequent trips to the nursery, woke up crying.

"What—? Just a minute." Emma called. She patted Andrea comfortingly even as she struggled to get up. Hurrying wasn't much of an option, but Emma went as fast as she could. The banging continued, and Andy was crying again.

She grabbed the door and opened it, anxious to stop the noise. "Please, ssh, the baby—Ryan!"

He strode past her without a word, crossing the small apartment quickly, heading for the nursery.

"Where is she?" he demanded as he came out of the small room. Before Emma could answer, he entered her bedroom. Emma tried to get to her room before him, but she couldn't move quickly, and trying made her dizzy. "Ryan, what are you doing? What's going on?"

He met her at the doorway, Andrea in his arms. "I'm taking my child back home. You're welcome to come if you want, but Andrea is going to be taken care of."

Panic rammed through Emma. He couldn't take her baby!

"I'm taking care of her!" she exclaimed. She put her hands on Andrea, trying to take her baby into her arms.

"You're too weak to even take care of yourself, much less Andrea. I'm keeping her safe."

He tried to move past her, but Emma wasn't going to let anyone take her baby. Especially Ryan.

As she tried to wrestle the baby free, the dizziness worsened, and she felt herself falling. The last thing she heard was Ryan's voice calling her name.

Chapter Five

Ryan freed one hand to grab Emma as she sank to the floor. He couldn't hold her, but he managed to break her fall. He laid her on the floor before returning Andrea to the bassinet in the nursery. Then he hurriedly carried Emma to the bed.

She didn't come to, as he'd hoped. Thoroughly panicked now, he grabbed the phone and called the doctor's office. His sense of urgency had the nurse passing the phone to the doctor at once.

"Steve, Emma passed out!" After a deep breath, he added, "She's not coming to."

"What happened?" his friend asked, his voice clipped.

Ryan didn't want to answer that question, but he had no choice. "She left the ranch. I came to take her back and we...argued."

"I'll be right there. You're at her apartment? Give me directions."

As soon as he hung up the phone, Ryan went back to check on Andrea, who was whimpering. He picked her up and carried her back into Emma's bedroom.

The bedroom where she'd been created.

Emma, her face pale, lay on the bed, not moving.

"Dear God, please let her be all right."

When he'd lost his wife and child, even though he'd felt guilty for surviving, he knew he'd done nothing to harm them. But now he knew that Emma's condition, whatever it was, was entirely his fault.

He cuddled the baby by Emma's side as he waited for the doctor. When he heard steps on the stairs he hurried to open the door.

"Where is she?" Steve demanded, not stopping.

"The room on the left," Ryan pointed out, on his heels.

Steve immediately took a small vial out and broke it, waving it beneath Emma's nose. Her eyelids fluttered. Then she finally opened them, and Ryan gave a sigh of relief.

Steve's voice gentled. "Emma, how are you?"

"I—don't know. Ryan—Ryan threatened to take Andrea!" she shrieked, trying to rise before she flopped back down on the bed.

"I'm here, Emma. Andrea's here, too."

Steve stared at him.

"She left the house today, and it's too soon. She can't take care of herself, much less the baby," he explained to Steve.

"Why did you leave, Emma?" Steve asked gently.

"I don't want to be there. I know when I'm not

wanted,'' she said, big tears rolling down her face. ''Please don't let him take my baby.''

Her pitiful plea made Ryan feel like a brute. ''I couldn't let the two of them try it on their own. Not yet,'' he insisted, trying to justify his behavior.

''Emma says you don't want her there,'' Steve pointed out.

''That's ridiculous. I've done everything I can to make sure she's taken care of.''

''Have you argued with her?''

''No! At least, not until now,'' Ryan assured him.

''He ignores us. He pretends we don't exist,'' Emma whispered. ''I had to stay in places like that when I was a child, but I don't now. My child will always be wanted!''

Steve looked at Ryan, waiting for his response, as if he were watching a tennis match.

''I thought that's what you wanted!'' Ryan roared. ''You didn't want me to touch either of you. Just to stay out of your way!''

Emma said nothing, turning her head away.

Ryan looked at Steve, at a loss as to what he should say or do.

After staring at him, Steve said, ''Emma, if Ryan promises to do a better job of making you feel welcome, would you go back to the ranch for a couple of more weeks? Would you give him a chance?''

Ryan panicked. He was afraid Emma would refuse. And afraid she would accept. Make her feel more welcome? He'd had Billy watch over the two of them. He'd hired Maria for around-the-clock care. What else could he do?

His blood ran cold as he realized the only other thing he could give her was himself. His company, his personal services. She'd hate that.

"He'd hate that," she whispered, still not looking at either him or Steve.

"Ryan?" Steve prodded.

He took a deep breath. "No, I—I wouldn't hate it. I was trying to do what I thought you wanted."

She closed her eyes and said nothing. Not exactly an enthusiastic endorsement.

"Emma, I promise I'll change. I don't hate your being there. I've—I've been checking on you every night. And—and I look at Andy while she sleeps." He took a deep breath. "I just want the two of you safe."

"I think you'll be better off if you give yourself a couple more weeks to heal," Steve said. "It wasn't easy here on your own, was it?"

After hesitating, Emma shook her head no.

"Why don't you let Ryan stay here tonight and take care of you two? Then, in the morning, he can take you home. That okay with you, Ryan?"

Ryan managed to swallow the protest that rose up. Stay here? In Emma's apartment, where they'd shared such pleasurable moments? But he had no choice. "Please, Emma?"

"Are you sure?" she asked, turning to look at him.

Her hazel eyes darkened with the emotion she was feeling. She wiped her wet cheeks as she waited for him to answer her.

There was only one answer. "I'm sure."

"Then, I guess...okay."

Steve stood. "Good girl. Get some rest now. It looks like Andrea has already gone to sleep." He tucked the covers around her, then motioned for Ryan to precede him out of the room.

"Don't you want to put Andrea in her crib?" Steve asked.

"No. I will in a minute." He didn't want to give up the warm bundle. Holding her made him feel better.

"You're getting a second chance, friend," Steve said, staring at him. "Can you handle it? You can't just shut the two of them out, pretend they don't exist."

Ryan couldn't discuss his fears even with Steve. So he nodded. Then he thanked his friend for his quick response.

"No problem. But I've got to get back to the office. I've got patients waiting."

After Steve left, Ryan tiptoed into the baby's room to tuck Andrea into the crib, then he stood beside it, staring at the baby.

He'd known he was getting too attached to Andy. Each night, as he'd stood by the bed, watching the baby sleep, he'd told himself he was just checking on her, but he'd known, whether he admitted it or not, that he'd fallen for Andy.

He also knew that spending time with Emma was going to cost him some heartache, too. But he had no choice.

He'd done his best to protect Merilee and Ryan, Jr. He could do no less for Emma and Andy. It didn't mean he'd love them. But he'd protect them, whatever the cost.

Andrea's cry awoke him hours later. He was sleeping on Emma's uncomfortable couch, and he rolled to his feet to see about the baby. As he got to the nursery, he remembered Emma had insisted he leave Andrea in her bed, so he didn't have to get up again.

He stepped to Emma's door, having left it open so he'd hear if she called. In the shadows, he stared at Emma, with Andrea already nursing. It was a beautiful picture, the loving mother feeding her child.

He knew she'd be upset if she realized he was watching, but he didn't think she could see him. Besides, all her attention was focused on her child. Their child.

He'd told his parents that they couldn't come over because Emma had had a setback. He didn't mention that her setback was that she'd run away because he had ignored her.

He knew Emma wouldn't complain to them. She'd never demanded anything of him. She wouldn't have this time if she hadn't been forced to agree to return. She'd been prepared to handle everything herself.

He shook his head. She was a strong, determined woman. Merilee had been strong, too, but she'd always wanted her way. She'd always wanted his attention.

Feeling guilty for even thinking such things about his wife, he backed away from the door so he couldn't see Emma and Andrea. He needed his sleep.

In the morning he'd take the pair back to the ranch. And tomorrow night his parents would visit.

He hadn't told Emma about that little complication.

He'd do that tomorrow. When they'd both had more sleep.

Emma woke at Andy's demand just after seven. With the baby right beside her, it didn't take much effort to feed her. And now that she knew she was returning to Ryan's ranch, where Billy would care for them, she felt a little more confident.

She wished she could have Maria again, too, but knowing Ryan was having to pay extra, she couldn't ask for Maria's assistance.

After she'd fed Andy, she burped the baby. Then she propped herself up against the pillows and talked baby nonsense to her daughter.

"Does she understand you?" Ryan asked, surprising her. He was leaning against the doorjamb, a small smile on his handsome face.

"Probably not. I'm sorry we awakened you."

"Don't worry about it," he muttered, rubbing his neck. "Your couch may be just fine as a couch, but as a bed, it lacks about two feet."

She apologized again, refraining from telling him it was his fault. She guessed she should bear some of the blame since she'd left without telling him.

"Are you hungry?" he asked.

She'd gotten spoiled at Ryan's. Billy's breakfasts were wonderful. "I'm afraid there's not much here for breakfast, but I can—"

"I didn't mean you should get up," Ryan insisted, taking several steps toward the bed, as if he needed to hold her down. "I'm calling Billy. I figure he should have breakfast ready about the time we get there, if you're ready to go?"

"Yes, I didn't get much unpacked last night."

"Good. I'll load the suitcases. You wrap up the baby and we're out of here. Can you manage that?"

"Yes," she agreed. It was amazing how much better she felt to be included in the planning. "But I'll have to get dressed."

"Oh, don't bother dressing. Just put on your robe," Ryan tossed over his shoulder as he headed to the baby's room.

She started to protest. Then she stopped. Why not? She could save her energy once again. She sat farther up and reached for the robe she'd left on the end of her bed. She slipped her arms into the sleeves and pulled it close around her. Then she gingerly slid to the edge of the bed and stood up.

Ryan strode past the bedroom door, the baby's things in his arms. Emma hoped he'd left a disposable diaper in the room so she could change Andy. To her relief, she discovered he'd left several. She freshened Andy, then wrapped her baby in a blanket. She took a second blanket, larger than the first one, to wrap her again.

It was spring in Wyoming, but that didn't mean warm. Most days it was in the forties, occasionally the fifties. Emma didn't want her baby catching a cold with all their traveling.

Once they were loaded in the car, Ryan carefully

drove them out of town. "Maria will be waiting for you," he said casually.

"No!"

He flicked her a glance before he turned his attention back to his driving. "You didn't get along with Maria?"

"Of course I got along with Maria. But I can manage. I don't want you paying any more money for— to take care of me."

He drove without speaking for several minutes. She wondered if he was mad at her again.

"Well, I think it will be cheaper to hire Maria than for me to stop working to take care of you. I can, of course, but—"

Emma was faced with a difficult decision. Let Ryan spend more money on her and Andy, or have him taking care of her twenty-four hours a day.

"I— All right, hire Maria. But I want you to keep track of the money you spend. I will pay you back." She had her pride.

"I've got a better idea. My grandfather was quite a reader. He left me his library, but I don't have the time to sort through it. I thought when you get feeling better, maybe you could design a library in one of the spare rooms and organize the books. I could pay you—"

"No!" Emma exclaimed again. "I'll be glad to do it, but I won't accept pay. I already owe you too much."

"Great. I've felt badly about not taking proper care of Gramps's legacy." He never looked at her, and she wondered if he was serious, or if he was making up things for her to do.

Which meant he understood her pride. A tiny glow, deep within her, warmed her all over.

When they reached the ranch, he got Andy from the carrier and put her in Emma's arms and lifted Emma from the seat, as he'd done last time.

"I can walk now, Ryan. I don't run any races, but—"

"No need for you to when I'm here. Neither of you weigh much. I'm going to have to accuse Billy of starving you to death."

It was a shock to realize he was teasing her. She rewarded his efforts with a tentative smile and mild protest. She hadn't done a lot of laughing in the past seven months.

Billy was holding open the back door and greeted her with enthusiasm.

Emma expected to be taken to bed at once, but, much to her surprise, Ryan sat her down in a chair at the big table in the kitchen.

"What are you doing?"

Ryan smiled at her. "We're going to be more social, remember? I'm going to take Andy to her bed, and then I'll come back and join you for breakfast. And Billy, don't let her eat my share before I get back."

Then he lifted the sleeping baby from her arms and left the kitchen. When she finally stopped staring at the door, she discovered Billy was as stunned by Ryan's actions as she was.

He looked at Emma. "Everything all right?"

How could she answer? "Uh, yes, Billy. The doctor decided I needed more care and—and Ryan offered to bring me back to the ranch. I hope I'm not causing you too much trouble."

"Heck, no. It's good to cook for someone who appreciates what I do. That bottomless pit never seems to care what I serve him," Billy said with a smile. "Besides, that little baby is so sweet, I was gonna miss her something fierce." He turned to the counter and set a large glass of milk in front of Emma.

Then, as he took plates kept warm in the oven and carried them to the table, Ryan came back in. "Grab a cup of coffee, Billy, and join us. Doc said it's time for Emma to be a little more social."

Billy's eyebrows rose, but he did as Ryan asked.

Ryan was relieved to have Emma and baby Andy back in his home. He wanted to be sure they were well-cared for, he assured himself. His mother always said life was more fun when there were babies—baby puppies, baby chicks, baby calves. And most especially real babies.

She was right.

But he was a little panicked about making conversation with Emma. That's why he was pleased that Billy joined them. Billy was a real talker. There wouldn't be any dead silences with him around.

Except for the one lingering on and on right now.

"Uh, this food is good, Billy," Ryan finally said, sending a message toward his cook pleading for help.

Billy obliged. "Glad you like it. Maria said she'd be along around nine."

"Oh, good. Did you tell her we'd just need her during the day? She'll be able to go home to Tommy in the evenings."

Emma looked up. "I'm glad. I think he'd been complaining a little about her being gone so much."

"Can't blame him, little Emma. A man likes to have his woman around."

Billy's wink and nod toward Ryan had Emma's cheeks turning to fire. She quickly ducked her head, staring at her breakfast.

"Billy, have there been any problems last night or this morning? Anything I need to check on once Maria gets here?" Ryan asked, hoping to change the subject.

"Nope, nary a one."

"Good. Emma, I thought I'd make a run into town. I think we're getting a little low on diapers. Is there anything you want? A book to read? Or I could rent some movies."

"Boss, we got plenty—" Billy began, but he stopped when Ryan kicked him under the table. "What did you do that for?"

"Sorry, Billy, I didn't know your foot was there," Ryan lied, avoiding his cook's stare.

"Well, as long as you're so set on going, why don't you stop by the grocery store and get some of that fancy decaffeinated coffee your mama likes? I discovered last night we're out of it. I made a fancy cake for their visit tonight and she'll want some."

All the color faded from Emma's cheeks. "Your parents are coming tonight?"

Well, he'd intended to break that news gently, after she'd had a good breakfast. But she'd only taken a couple of bites before Billy spilled the beans.

"I'm not sure that's a good idea," Emma said, staring at Ryan.

Billy frowned. "They're fine people, Emma. And they'll love little Andy."

But they wouldn't love what she'd done to their son. The first time she'd met them, his mother had taken her aside to express her appreciation for Emma's dragging Ryan out of his mourning.

But Emma was pretty sure having his baby and keeping her a secret wasn't what his mother had in mind.

"I think it would be better if I didn't see them," she said, hating the way her voice shook.

"We'll talk about it later, after you've finished your breakfast and gotten back in bed," Ryan said, glaring at Billy.

"I'm not hungry," she murmured, staring at her food in dismay. A few minutes ago, she'd been hungry. Now she wanted to crawl in a hole and never come out.

"I knew Billy was starving you to death. I ought to fire you, you miserable old cur," Ryan threatened, winking his right eye, the one Emma couldn't see.

"Aw, Emma, eat something else so I can keep my job," Billy pleaded. But he overdid his acting.

"You're a fraud, Billy," Emma protested. "You both are. You know Ryan isn't going to fire you."

"You never can tell," the old man insisted. "Just to be on the safe side, can't you eat a few more bites?" Then, as she picked up her fork, he launched into a long wandering tale about a time Ryan supposedly threatened to fire him.

Ryan ate his breakfast as Billy talked. Somehow, Emma found herself doing the same, almost forgetting the fact that her baby's grandparents were coming over to see her this evening.

She hoped they'd be gentle. They could ignore her, as she figured she deserved, but she wanted Andy to have it all…for as long as she could.

Chapter Six

Much to Emma's surprise, after breakfast Ryan apologized for not coming in for lunch, explaining that he had to go to the far pasture, and he wouldn't get back for the middle meal of the day.

"I don't expect that, Ryan. The doctor didn't mean you had to give up your job. Just—just occasionally speak," Emma said, her cheeks bright red as Billy stared at both of them.

"Yeah," Ryan said, not looking at her. "I'll be here for dinner, though. Mom and Dad are coming for dessert. Take a nap this afternoon so you'll be rested."

Billy didn't hesitate to speak his mind. "Who died and made you king?"

Ryan had been on his way out the door. Coming to an abrupt halt, he faced his cook. "What are you talking about?"

"You're giving Emma orders like she don't have any sense at all."

Ryan glared at Billy. "I'm trying to take care of her, like Steve said. She needs to rest."

"I reckon she knows that. Don't you be chasing her off again." Billy stood and began clearing the table.

Emma stared at the two men, unable to believe they were about to fight over whether or not she took a nap. "Please…Billy, I *will* need a nap. Ryan is trying to show concern about my well-being. The doctor said—"

"I don't need your protection, Emma!" Ryan ripped back.

"Then I don't need your concern. In fact, I don't need to be here. Billy—"

"Don't you dare leave!" Ryan roared.

"There you go again, giving orders. She don't belong to you. You haven't married her in spite of giving her a baby." Billy stacked the dishes in the sink, not looking at his boss.

"Now I really am going to fire you, old man," Ryan roared again.

Emma leaped to her feet, intending to intervene before someone said something that couldn't be taken back. But as before when she moved too quickly, she grew dizzy. A moan escaped her, startling Ryan, and he grabbed her before she hit the floor.

"Damn it! You don't have any sense at all. You can't go jumping around like that," Ryan protested and he carried her down the hall to her bedroom.

"I didn't want you and Billy fighting," she whispered.

"Wouldn't be the first time," Billy muttered, following Ryan.

Ryan lowered her onto the bed. "We won't fight anymore," he said gruffly. "We're both trying to protect you, each in his own way."

"Please, I'm fine. I promise," she said, looking first at Ryan, and then Billy.

Ryan backed away from the bed, glad Billy was behind him. It stopped him from kissing her. He wanted to reassure her of his—concern. Yeah, that was it. Concern.

"Uh, I've got to go to work," he said, staring at her. "Billy and I will get out of here and let you sleep. Maria should be here soon."

Her gentle smile was almost his undoing. She was blaming herself, he could tell.

Billy followed him back into the kitchen.

"Billy—"

"Boss—"

They both stopped and stared at each other until he waved for Billy to go first.

"I shouldn't have interfered," Billy said, ducking his head.

"Hell, Billy, I shouldn't have let it get to me. You know you'll always have a job here. I'd never find such a good cook anywhere else."

"That's true," the old cowboy said, raising his chin. "But you haven't been doing right by Emma."

Ryan sighed and rubbed the back of his neck. "I'm trying, Billy."

"Now, you are. But what you said to her—"

"When?" he asked, frowning, hoping Billy didn't mean what he feared he did.

"When you sent her away."

"Damn!" Ryan muttered. "Look, Billy, she surprised me—I wasn't prepared to—to give up Merilee and Ryan, Jr. Afterward I wanted to apologize, but I was afraid she'd think I'd changed my mind. So I didn't. But I had no idea she was pregnant."

"You didn't?"

"No." He didn't say anything else, but Billy's words explained his attitude the last few months. He'd been crustier than ever, barely speaking to him.

The cook sighed. "Then, okay. But she's a good woman, boss. You be sure you treat her right. Last week—"

"She hates me, Billy. I thought she wanted me to stay away from her. But it made her feel unwanted. I'm trying to find a middle ground here. So we'll be sharing our meals when possible. Wait dinner for me tonight."

"Right, boss," Billy agreed, a smile on his face.

Ryan got out of there before Billy asked any questions.

In spite of her long nap, Emma wasn't feeling more rested that evening. She and Maria had bathed Andy and dressed her in a clean nightgown, which was all she had there for her little girl.

She'd bought several little terrycloth footed suits

for her baby, but they were at her apartment. In all the emotional turmoil when she'd returned to the apartment, she'd forgotten to pick them up.

She knew Ryan had come home a little while ago, but then he'd left at once to go to the store. Maria had gone home to her husband, and Emma looked at her bed longingly. It was tempting to crawl in and cover up her head.

But she wasn't a coward. So, she gathered up a clean nightgown and her robe and headed for the bathroom for a shower. By the time she'd finished, she was shaking again from exhaustion. She was glad she hadn't decided to dress up for her guests.

When she came out of the bathroom, her hair blown dry but not styled, Ryan was waiting.

"Are you okay?"

She nodded, not mentioning her trembling legs.

"You look like hell!" he muttered and scooped her up into his arms.

"Thank you," she said stiffly, refusing to relax against him.

"I didn't mean—you're pale as a ghost. Didn't you get any rest?"

"Yes, I took a nap. I just need to sit down a few minutes. Then I'll be fine."

"Do you want to take another nap or are you ready for dinner? Billy's got it ready." He'd stopped walking, waiting for her answer.

"I'm ready for dinner. It will make me stronger. I'm sorry I didn't dress, but—"

"Don't be silly," he growled and reversed his direction.

"I can walk to the kitchen, Ryan. I've been managing all day."

After settling her in a chair at the table and telling Billy they were ready to eat, he stared at her. "So, that's the problem? You've been doing too much." He glared at Billy.

"Don't look at me," Billy protested. "She said she was okay."

"No, please don't fight! Please."

Billy grinned, surprising her. "Not to worry. We've been fighting ever since he was six years old. He was even big for his britches back then."

Ryan, obviously making an effort, too, said, "He wouldn't let me have all the cookies I wanted."

"Couldn't bake that many," Billy returned. "Now, you, Emma darlin', can have whatever you want. Just tell me."

"I knew you favored her," Ryan protested, grinning.

Emma raised a hand. "Okay, okay, I believe you. You don't have to work so hard at convincing me."

Ryan exchanged a rueful grin with his cook. "Guess we're not too good at this acting thing."

Emma smiled at both of them. She couldn't believe the difference in Ryan's behavior. Even when they'd been having an affair, he'd tried to maintain his mourning. Of course, she hadn't known his story then. She'd thought he was normally morose. "You'll do. Something smells wonderful, Billy."

"That's my girl," Billy said, a big grin on his face. "I made pot roast. Lots of iron. Good vegetables, too."

He quickly brought the dishes to the table and they all ate. Emma had noticed before that there wasn't a lot of conversation at the dinner table. Everyone on the ranch worked hard and didn't waste time when it came to eating.

It didn't take long for Emma's appetite to dwindle, and she sat silently, watching the other two eat. She'd like to go back to bed, but she knew they would protest and stop eating themselves.

Ryan happened to look up and noticed her hands folded together on the table.

"Why aren't you eating?"

"I have eaten, and it was delicious." She smiled at Billy.

"You need to eat more."

She stiffened at his dictatorial tones, then forced her shoulders to relax. "My appetite is small right now. It will grow, though. Then I'll have to go on a diet."

His gaze roved over her body, and she could almost feel his touch, sending shivers all over her. "I doubt that. When you were pregnant—" he broke off and looked away "—did you gain a lot of weight?" he finally asked.

She didn't want to talk about her pregnancy, but it was an innocent question. "I was sick a lot, throwing up, so no, I didn't gain much weight."

"Is that why Andrea is so small?" he asked.

She stiffened again. "I did the best I could."

"I didn't mean—I wasn't criticizing you!" Ryan hurriedly said. "It's just that Jackson is a lot bigger."

Emma sighed. "She came two weeks early. I think

it was because of my high blood pressure. It couldn't have been the diabetes."

"You're diabetic?" Billy asked in alarm. "But I baked a cake."

"I had gestational diabetes, Billy. I'm fine now. They checked me before I left the hospital," she explained hurriedly.

With a frown on his face, he said, "That's good. But I'll watch what I cook from now on. I can find some sugar-free recipes and—"

"Billy, I'm fine. Neither of you needs to worry about me. I'm getting stronger all the time. And you're both being perfect gentlemen about having me shoved on you. I appreciate it." She looked at Ryan, understanding how hard he was trying to do what he'd promised.

If anything, he was overdoing it. She didn't want to make him miserable. And Billy was just as bad.

"You're not causing any problems," Ryan assured her. "Can't you eat a little more roast?"

With exasperation, she refused. "No. I'm saving room for Billy's cake."

Both men opened their mouths, and she held up a hand. "Not a word. I'm fine. In fact, Billy, I could go ahead and start on the dishes. I know you want them cleared away before our company comes." She tried to make sure she didn't give away how nervous she was, but her voice trembled a little.

"You touch a dish and I'll tan your hide," Billy returned, surprising her.

Emma couldn't resist teasing him. "And you complained about Ryan's behavior? At least he didn't threaten to beat me.''

"Aw, Emma, I was just teasing. But you don't need to be doing my job," Billy protested earnestly.

"And there's nothing to make you nervous about my parents' visit, honey. They mostly want to see the baby. My mother loves babies," Ryan added.

Obviously she hadn't fooled him.

"Of course," she said, looking away. His blue eyes showed concern, and she had to fight the desire to believe he really cared about her.

As the two men finished, the phone rang.

Ryan answered it. By the brief conversation, Emma knew the caller was his mother. When he hung up the phone, he confirmed her suspicion. "That was Mom. They'll be here in a few minutes."

"I'll get started on the dishes and making that coffee," Billy said. "Take Emma into the den so she can relax."

"Now who's the dictator?" Ryan asked before he scooped Emma into his arms.

"I can walk."

"Save your energy for visiting," he told her.

Which only made her more nervous.

Ryan heard a car outside and stood. Emma flashed a look at him, panic in her hazel eyes.

He'd tried to reassure her. In actuality, she had less to worry about than he did. His parents wanted to "talk" after they saw the baby. He knew the "talk" would be an examination of his intentions.

He was having enough trouble with Steve's instructions. Not that being friendly to Emma was hard. Just by her quiet, undemanding behavior, her soft beauty, her smile, she invited kindness. He could handle kindness. He wasn't normally a mean person.

But it also meant opening up. Exposing his weaknesses. One of his weaknesses was the yearning he felt for Emma. He'd been able to keep the wanting at bay after she'd left because he'd shut everything about Emma Davenport out of his mind.

He couldn't do that when he had to share his home, his time, even his thoughts, with her.

"Anybody home?" he heard his mother call.

"Wait here," he ordered and hurried to the kitchen.

"Hi, Mom, Dad," he said and hugged his parents. He'd missed them since they'd moved. "Glad you're back home."

"We're thrilled to be back, especially for such happy reasons. Where are Emma and the baby?" his mother demanded, her face eager.

"Emma's in the den. Come on in and say hi. Then I'll see if Andy is ready for her debut."

"Beth says she's little," Leigh Nix said even as she followed Ryan into the other room.

Billy was fixing a tray of cake and coffee, after having greeted the couple. "She's perfect!" he exclaimed, frowning. "Sweetest little thing you've ever seen."

Ryan cleared his throat. "She's smaller than Jackson, but Emma said she came a little early."

He stood back when they reached the den, carefully watching his parents' reactions to Emma. Leigh sailed past him, her arms extended for a hug with Emma. His father followed her and bent down and kissed Emma's cheeks after his wife had hugged her.

Emma appeared stunned by their friendliness, but Ryan wasn't surprised. His parents were good people. It wasn't Emma who was going to have to have a "talk."

"Ryan, can you go see if Andrea can visit?" his mother asked eagerly. "My first granddaughter! Why, I don't even know her complete name!" She looked at Emma expectantly.

Emma stared at Ryan, saying nothing.

He knew what was wrong. She didn't want to say Andy's middle name after he'd accused her of trying to get his mother on her side. "Emma named her Andrea Leigh. Mostly we call her Andy."

"You named her after me?" Leigh Nix asked, startled.

"I hope you don't mind. You're her only grandmother, and I—I wanted her to feel she had a family."

Though his parents had met Emma when they were dating, during a visit they'd made in the summer, they didn't really know much about her. His father asked, "Is your own mother dead?"

Emma raised her chin slightly and said, "I don't know. I was abandoned at birth."

His parents turned to stare at Ryan, as if asking why he hadn't prepared them. He shrugged his shoulders.

"So you were adopted?" Leigh asked.

Emma shook her head. "I was sick when I was a

baby. Afterwards, I—I was never chosen.'' She paused, then said, ''I apologize for not letting Ryan…and you…know about Andrea until now, but I had a difficult pregnancy and I didn't have the strength to deal with much of anything.''

It was his father who responded. He had sat down on the couch with his wife, near Emma, and he reached over to pat her hand. ''We understand. Ryan said you had a hard time. Are you feeling better now?''

Emma's lips trembled as she tried to smile. ''I'm getting stronger. I hope I'll be able to manage on my own in a couple of weeks, so I won't have to take advantage of Ryan's generosity.''

It was time to change the subject before his parents said more than they should. ''I'll see if Andy is awake. Mom, you want to help me?''

He'd known that would get his mother's attention. He only hoped his father wouldn't say anything.

Emma was overwhelmed by the kindness of Ryan's parents. If someone had kept her grandchild from her, she wouldn't have been as tolerant.

She watched Ryan and his mother hurry from the room. When she flicked a look at Mr. Nix, she hurriedly looked away. She didn't know what to say.

''Don't worry about Ryan taking care of you, Emma,'' he said quietly. ''That's his responsibility.''

''No,'' she said, raising her chin. ''He didn't ask for—for a child. He doesn't want a family. I'll take care of my child.''

Before he could respond, Leigh Nix came into the room, holding Andrea in her arms.

"Oh, Joe, look at the little darling! She's so delicate, so beautiful. And she has hair! Jackson doesn't have much at all."

Emma avoided Ryan's gaze and kept hers on her child. Not that she didn't trust Ryan's folks with her child. She did. But it was a new experience to share her baby with them.

Andy stretched as Leigh sat down with her. Then she slowly opened her eyes. Leigh gasped. "I think she has blue eyes! Don't you, Joe?"

Emma felt a nudge of resentment. It was as if they were cataloguing proof that Andy was Ryan's child.

"But she definitely has your hair, Emma," Joe Nix said. "It's much darker than Ryan's. Why, when he was born he was blond."

Emma tried to smile, but she was growing more tense by the moment. "Yes," she murmured.

At the sound of her voice, the baby turned her head toward Emma.

"Look! She already recognizes your voice, Emma. Oh, my, she's such a darling," Leigh exclaimed.

Billy entered with the dessert and coffee he'd prepared. "So, she's up, is she?" he asked, grinning. "She's such a good baby."

"Are you taking care of her, Billy?" Joe asked. "Do you have any help?"

"Maria, Tommy's wife, has been coming over every day," Ryan hurriedly assured his parents. "At first, she stayed twenty-four hours a day, but now she goes home before dinner." He didn't mention that their new schedule was only in its first day.

Emma kept quiet. She decided the less she said, the better. Besides, all the tension was exhausting her energy. She longed to go to bed, taking her baby with her.

"She seems so tiny," Leigh said, unwrapping her blanket to examine every inch of her grandchild. "Especially compared to Jackson. Is she gaining weight?" she asked Emma.

"Yes, she has a good appetite. She's gained almost four ounces above her birth weight." She knew that didn't sound like much but the doctor had assured her that was good. But she'd forgotten she was talking to an experienced mother.

"Oh, that's excellent. Jackson hasn't been eating as well. That's more than he's gained."

"Is Beth all right?" Emma asked, concern in her voice. "She seemed to be doing well at the hospital."

"Oh, she's doing fine. And Jackson is now, too. Steve said some babies have to adjust to breast-feeding. You are breast-feeding, too, aren't you? It's much better for the baby, you know."

Emma nodded, but Ryan said, "Mom, Emma is a great mother."

"Of course, dear," Leigh returned. "But some new mothers prefer to use bottles. I just wondered."

Emma swallowed and tried to sit up straighter. She was feeling her energy drain away.

"My wife didn't mean any criticism, Emma," Joe said gently. "In fact, we don't have any questions about how things have gone so far. Our main question is—when is the wedding?''

Emma stared at the man before her gaze flickered to Ryan's face. He didn't seem surprised by his father's question.

''Mr. Nix, I—'' she started, feeling it was her fault Ryan had been put in this position.

''Dad, can we discuss this later? Emma is tired. Let me get her settled while you enjoy the cake Billy made. Then I'll come back and we can...talk.''

He sounded like he intended to tuck her in bed, like it was something he did every night. Emma stared at him, longing for bed but afraid to leave him alone to face his parents' questions.

''No, I need to explain to your parents that we're not getting married,'' she said hurriedly. ''I don't expect—''

Joe Nix interrupted. ''Well, you damn well should!''

Chapter Seven

A strained silence followed Joe's roar.

Then to Emma's surprise, Ryan strode to the sofa, scooped her into his arms and walked out of the room.

"Ryan, what are you doing? We have to explain to your parents that we're not getting married," she said, trying to remain stiff in his strong arms.

"They're my parents. You don't have to explain anything. I'll take care of it."

She could tell he was upset. She was, too. He'd made it clear she wasn't—and never would be—a part of his family. Fair enough. He'd made it clear she wasn't wanted. Her foolish heart never seemed to give up, however.

You have a family now, she reminded herself. *You and Andrea are a family. That's enough.* It would have to be. "I'm sorry to cause you so much grief. When I move away—"

He lowered her to the bed. "Don't worry about it, honey. Just get some rest. You're trying to do too much too soon."

She pressed her lips together and looked away from him. "Andy. I'll probably need to feed her soon."

"When she's ready, I'll bring her in. I think my mother would like to hold her as long as she can. Is that all right?"

She appreciated his asking instead of demanding. With a nod, she tried smiling. It probably wasn't her best effort, but she really was tired.

He surprised her even more by bending over and kissing her cheek.

She stared as he hurried out of the room. Casual caresses were a rare occurrence in her life. Even when they'd been sleeping together, Ryan hadn't touched her unless they were making love—having sex.

It wouldn't be that way for Andy, she vowed, cradling her cheek in her hand. She'd store up memories of these rare moments with Ryan before she left. She'd make sure Andy felt her love in kisses and hugs, even if it was just the two of them.

With a deep sigh, she closed her eyes, still touching the skin where Ryan's lips had been.

Ryan returned to the den, angry with his parents. He hadn't wanted them to upset Emma. He'd known he'd have to explain what was going on—as much as he could—but Emma wasn't used to family dynamics. She wasn't well enough for arguments, even though she'd tried.

Billy was still in the den, talking to his parents when he came in. But all conversation stopped and the three of them stared at him.

"What's going on here, son?" Joe asked, irritation in his voice. "Emma's a lady. How could you treat her that way?"

He'd known his father would condemn his behavior. Hell, he did himself. He sat down and cleared his throat. "I know I shouldn't have—Emma and I had—I didn't know she was pregnant."

"You can't tell when a woman's about to give birth?" his father asked, his voice rising.

"Not if I haven't seen her for seven months!" he snapped in return.

That response stopped the conversation.

Then his mother, with a frown, said, "We were here last September, and Beth introduced me to Emma. I was so happy you'd finally adjusted to Merilee and Ryan, Jr.'s deaths. When did you stop seeing Emma? And why?"

Billy stood up. "I'll take this stuff to the kitchen," he said, waving to the dirty dishes. "Anyone need more coffee?"

"Chicken," Ryan muttered under his breath. Not that he thought Billy could deter his parents' criticism. Or would even want to. He was definitely fond of Emma.

His parents said nothing as Billy gathered the dirty dishes and hurried from the room.

Ryan looked at his parents. Then he clasped his

hands between his legs, his arms resting on his knees, and began his confession.

"I'm not proud of what I did. But I didn't intend to hurt Emma. We—became friends. I sensed a loneliness in her that matched my own. We'd have dinner together a couple of times a week and talk. Then one night I went back to her apartment to talk more. And—one thing led to another."

He drew a deep breath, sneaking a look at his parents. Their expressions were unreadable. He dropped his gaze to the floor again. "I was shocked by what had happened. I'd never intended—Merilee was still in my heart. But what I had with Emma was—good. So I didn't stop."

"Understandable," his father muttered.

"Yeah, well, early October, Emma came out to the ranch on a Saturday. We had dinner together and were going to watch a movie. She seemed a little edgy, which was unusual. When I questioned her, she suggested we live together, have a family."

He couldn't sit still and explain his despicable behavior. He rose and began to pace the floor. "I knew then I'd made a huge mistake. I fell apart, yelling at her that I'd never have another family. That I loved Merilee, that Ryan, Jr. had been the light of my life. No one could replace either of them." He drew another deep breath. "I was cruel, but I didn't intend to be. I just lost control. She ran away."

"Did you apologize?" Leigh asked softly.

He shook his head and stared out into the night. "I know I should've, but I was afraid she'd believe I would change my mind. I rationalized it would be better for her to move on, to find someone else, because she really is—special."

"But surely you saw her around town, noticed she'd gained weight, at least," his mother said.

"It was winter. Everyone was bundled up. I never went back to the library. I saw her from a distance, once or twice, but mostly I avoided going into town. I asked Beth about her, because they'd been friends, but Beth had only seen her once, right after our—talk. She said Emma had refused to continue their friendship."

"Wasn't there talk in the town?" his father questioned.

He shook his head no. "Emma dropped out of sight. She didn't go to church anymore. She kept her coat on at the grocery store. She drove to Buffalo for her prenatal visits."

"So how did you find out?" His father's voice was gruff.

"I found out when I went to the hospital to see Jackson the day he was born." He closed his eyes, picturing the moment that had changed his life.

"Emma called you? From the hospital?" Her mother was frowning, and he knew she was getting upset with Emma.

"No. I saw my name on the birth card when the nurse brought Andy in."

"Oh, Emma should have told you, Ryan. That was wrong of her."

He smiled at his mother, having known she would be on his side. But he couldn't allow her to feel that way. "She was going to tell me. But she had a rough pregnancy and the delivery didn't go well. She's improved a lot since then, but she was facing a return to work and no money. She was frightened. And I'd been vicious the last time we'd talked.''

"Then why tell *anyone?*" his father asked. "Was she trying to ruin your reputation?''

Ryan put his hands behind his back and faced his parents. "Emma told you she was an orphan. She never knew who her parents were. She'd never do that to her child. I don't think she realized they would put that information on the card. She just wanted her child to *know,* as she didn't.''

"Oh, the poor child,'' Leigh said, her heart in Emma's corner suddenly.

"So what's she doing here if you're not going to marry?''

"Dad, she had no money, no one to help her. She could barely stand—and then for no more than a minute without collapsing. I had to take care of her…and Andy. I insisted she come here to recover. She fought me all the way, but she didn't have much choice.

"I thought once I got her here, we'd work something out, but she was so angry. I decided she wanted me to stay away. So I did. Then yesterday, she got Maria to take her back to town.''

"But it's too soon,'' his mother exclaimed.

"Yeah. I went to get her. Had to call Steve because she fainted. She said she wouldn't stay where neither she nor Andy were wanted.''

"Oh,'' Leigh moaned.

"Yeah, so I promised I'd be friendlier, that I wanted them on the ranch."

"You going to convince her to stay?" Joe demanded, staring at Ryan.

"I'm going to try. She's talking about moving away, but I'm hoping to convince her to stay."

His mother leaned forward eagerly. "But if you love her, you—"

Ryan froze. Then he roared, "I didn't say that!"

The baby, having rested quietly in Leigh's arms, whimpered. Ryan reached for his daughter, but Leigh pressed her closer.

"You're scaring her!" she protested.

"I didn't mean to. Give her to me." He took his child and cradled her against him, murmuring soothing words. Andy settled down at once, her eyes open, staring at him.

"Ryan, you can't—you mustn't let Emma and the baby leave," his mother protested. "Andy's your daughter. What if Emma needs help? Or the baby gets sick? Would she call you?"

Ryan didn't have to ask Emma those questions. He knew the answer already. No, she wouldn't call. She wouldn't ask for help. If he let her and Andy leave, she'd never come back.

He stared at his child's beautiful little face, held her warmth against him. He'd avoided thinking about the future since he'd retrieved Emma and the baby this morning. He'd told himself he would handle things one day at a time.

But his mother was forcing him to face the future. And he didn't like it.

"Emma doesn't understand the importance of family, Ryan. You've got to insist that she stay."

He thought his mother was wrong. From things Emma had said in the past, he believed she understood the importance of family more than anyone, because she'd never had one.

His father followed. "We'll check with Jack, but if you're not married, I don't think you have any rights about the baby. You need to marry her."

He stared at his father. His words sounded so cold, so...legal. He wanted Emma to be happy, protected, not alone anymore.

He could picture Emma with quiet contentment on her face. She'd looked that way after they made love. Merilee had expected to be loved, to be treasured. Emma had always been grateful, as if it was unexpected, he realized.

His behavior seemed even more heinous, now, as he remembered Emma's reactions.

He hadn't realized his parents had stood until his father spoke again. "We'll go back to Beth's and let you take care of your daughter," he said, gesturing to Andy. "And I'll let you know what Jack says."

Ryan wanted to protest any planned legal action against Emma. That would be impossible. But he couldn't face losing contact with his child, either. He nodded his head, saying nothing.

His parents both stepped closer and kissed the baby, then hugged him and said goodbye.

Ryan remained in place, holding Andy, for quite a while after they'd gone. He couldn't imagine going back to his lonely existence without Emma and the baby. Even the week before, when he'd hidden from their presence, he'd thought of them all day. He'd checked on the baby each night. He'd asked Billy questions about Emma.

Now he realized his world had revolved around the two of them, even if he hadn't spent time with them. Today, having shared meals with Emma, having introduced his daughter to his parents, holding her now, he realized he couldn't give them up.

What was he going to do?

Twice in the night, Emma was awakened by Andy's demand for food. The first time she struggled to get out of bed, after remembering that Maria wasn't there to bring her baby to her. Before she could get upright, however, Ryan had appeared in the doorway, Andy in his arms.

"No need to get up," he said softly, and placed her baby in her arms.

Emma stared at him, trying to gather her thoughts. Did he expect her to feed Andy in front of him?

As if he read her mind, he said, "I'll be in the den. Just call when she's ready to go back to bed." Then he disappeared.

When she looked at her watch and realized it was almost midnight, she decided he must've still been up, reading, though it was late since he'd be up at six.

Then Andy claimed her attention and she concentrated on feeding her child. Afterwards, she covered herself and softly called for Ryan.

With a smile, he took Andy back to her bassinet.

Emma lay there, hearing the rustling of the blanket as he covered her child. Then silence. She was listening for his footsteps climbing the stairs, but she fell asleep before she heard them.

At four, they repeated the process, Ryan again appearing before she could leave the bed, Andy in his arms. "She's really hungry this time," he announced with a sleepy grin. "Or I was sleeping deeper."

Andy was complaining with all her tiny might.

"She probably needs a change," Emma said, rubbing her eyes.

"I should've thought of that. We'll be right back."

She blinked as he reversed his direction and disappeared from view. Emma heard him talking to Andy and the baby's screams lessened to soft whimpers. Then he returned to her bedroom.

"She's ready to eat, Mama," he said and handed the baby to her.

"Thank you. I could've changed her."

He shrugged his shoulders and turned to leave.

"Ryan? How did you hear her from upstairs?"

"I was in the den," he told her. Then he was gone.

Emma thought about what he'd said. Had he fallen asleep reading? He was going to be very tired in the morning. Maybe she should start letting Andy sleep with her. That way the baby wouldn't wake Ryan up.

After Andy was satisfied, Emma decided she should put her baby to bed without disturbing Ryan. He'd probably gone to bed anyway. Shoving the covers back, not bothering with a robe, she stood, then reached for Andy, lying on the bed.

"Why didn't you call me?" Ryan demanded from the door.

Emma spun around so quickly, she almost fell over. Ryan was at her elbow at once, supporting her. "Back into bed before you pass out," he ordered sternly. He took Andy from her and held the cover for Emma to return to bed.

"But you're not getting any sleep."

"Neither are you," he pointed out. Then he leaned down and kissed her cheek again before he and the baby left the room.

She closed her eyes. Those sweet touches could get to be a habit, she decided. One that she needed to avoid. Sadness filled her even as sleep overcame her thoughts.

Ryan hurried into the kitchen. "Have you heard Emma or the baby?" he asked Billy.

"Not a peep."

"Okay, well, have breakfast ready in about ten minutes. I'm going to clean up and then I'll check on them."

"You bet, boss," Billy said with a grin.

Ryan hadn't been sure Billy would agree with his new schedule. Not that Billy's agreement would change his mind, but it meant a little extra work for the man. Ryan had decided to get up at his regular time, have a cup of coffee, then go do chores at the barn until Emma woke up.

He'd come back to the house for breakfast with her before he went out for the day.

After washing up, he tiptoed down the hall to

Emma's bedroom. Instead of knocking, he opened the door and peeked in. Emma was still sound asleep, relaxed under the cover.

The sudden urge to join her, to press sweet kisses to her soft lips to awaken her, filled him. He took a step back in protest. He and Emma weren't lovers anymore. They weren't a married couple. They weren't anything.

Well, that wasn't true. He was her caregiver right now. And the father of her baby.

As if on cue, Andy let out a wail. Ryan hurried out of Emma's room before she could realize he'd been watching her. This time he changed the baby before he brought her back to Emma.

"What are you doing here?" Emma asked as soon as he entered her room. "It's after eight o'clock."

He grinned. "I came back after doing some chores to have breakfast with you."

She frowned. "Ryan, I didn't mean you had to change your life to wait on me. And we need to talk about last night, too."

Andy began fussing again.

Ryan handed her to Emma. "Feed this insistent little lady. Then we'll have breakfast together and discuss whatever you want." He slipped from the room before she could protest.

He headed for the kitchen where Billy was taking biscuits from the oven. "Need any help? Emma is feeding the baby."

"Pour some milk for Emma, why don't you? She needs to drink lots of milk while she's nursing."

"Don't tell me you read a book on nursing, too," Ryan protested as he did as Billy asked.

"Nope. But your mother told me last night. And no caffeine, either. But I made some of that coffee you bought for last night."

Ryan frowned. "That's not what I had this morning, is it? Is that why I'm still sleepy? No caffeine?"

"Nah!" Billy said with a grin. "I'd still be asleep without a jolt of live coffee."

"If you're sleepy," Emma said from the doorway, frowning at him, "it's because you got up and down all night with Andy."

He ignored those words and hurried to her side. "Come sit down. Did the baby go back to sleep?"

"Yes. But you mustn't get up at night with the baby. You can't do that and work all day, too, Ryan. With or without caffeine."

Billy set the plate of biscuits on the table. "Come on and eat while everything's hot." He joined Emma at the table and stared at Ryan, still standing beside her.

Ryan slid into the chair next to Emma and passed the biscuits to her. Then he put scrambled eggs on her plate and added some bacon.

"Ryan, I can serve myself. I'm not Andy!" she exclaimed.

"Sorry, honey, but I'm starving. This way was faster." He wasn't sure she believed him, but his explanation stopped her complaining.

In fact, she left him in peace to eat his breakfast, only occasionally speaking to Billy. However, when

he leaned back in his chair with a sigh of contentment, she tried again.

"Did you sleep in the den all night?"

"Yeah. Billy, how about another cup of coffee.
Emma, Billy made some caffeine-free coffee for you,
too. Want some?"

"Yes, please. And quit trying to change the subject," she said firmly, after nodding to Billy.

"I'm not. I was trying to think of your comfort."

"Did you sleep on the sofa? If I remember cor-
rectly, the last time you had to do that, you protested."

Billy jumped up from the table. "Uh, I think I'll
start some laundry and clean the dishes later." He
hurried from the kitchen as if he were being chased.

"I think you embarrassed Billy," Ryan said with
a grin. "Shame on you, Emma."

"I was talking about two nights ago when you
came to my apartment!" she exclaimed, her cheeks
turning red, making her look delightful.

"I know," he said, still smiling, "but Billy
doesn't know that."

"Ryan, you're trying to distract me again. Why
weren't you upstairs sleeping?"

"Because you and Andy needed me," he replied
simply, daring her with his gaze to contradict him.

Chapter Eight

Emma narrowed her eyes as she stared at Ryan. "I'm getting better, Ryan. I just need a little help with the housework and cooking. It's not necessary to rearrange your entire schedule."

Her words didn't seem to faze him as he sipped his coffee. "So the way things were last week is how you want it?"

Emma realized she'd boxed herself in. No, she couldn't stay here if things went back to the sterile existence of last week. But it was dangerous to have him too close. For either her or Andy, because in a few weeks, he wouldn't be around.

"I needed to know you didn't mind my being here. But I don't want to disrupt your life."

"You want that last piece of bacon?" he asked, as if she'd said the weather was nice.

"No," she snapped. "Are you listening to me?"

"Every word," he assured her, considering the bacon before taking a bite.

You'd think he was having his last meal! She huffed as she watched him. He was a sight to behold, his handsome face, broad shoulders, slim hips. All man.

And sweet.

Not many men would change their entire schedule to accommodate a woman who meant nothing to them.

"Ryan, I want you to know this isn't necessary."

"You're wrong, honey. Breakfast is the most important meal of the day."

Emma was always patient, always kind, slow to anger, but she slapped her hand down on the table hard enough to make the orange-juice glasses jump.

"Ryan Nix, you're not being serious!"

"Whoa. Calm down, Emma," he said and reached for her hand.

His touch calmed her at once, which irritated her even more. She yanked her hand away.

"Look, Emma, I want you to tell me if I do something that upsets you, but I'm only trying to do what the doctor said. And...I'm actually enjoying it."

"You needn't sound so surprised!" she snapped again.

"Mercy, honey, I can't get it right this morning."

Much to Emma's mortification, tears pooled in her eyes and she ducked her head. What was wrong with her? "I didn't mean to complain. But last night—"

"Ah, I was afraid we'd have to discuss last night."

"Were they—do they hate me?" Her voice shook,

but the thought that she'd caused problems for Ryan in his family was horrible.

Ryan pushed back from the table, surprise on his face. "Hate you? Why would they?"

"Ryan, I'm sure the entire town is talking about—about me. You didn't want either one of us, and I made it so you couldn't ignore us."

He took her hand again. "I want to take care of both of you, Emma. Don't doubt that. My parents were disappointed by the situation. And they wanted to be sure I was being responsible." He paused before drawing her hand to his lips for a brief caress. "And they want to know what we're going to do."

"About the gossip? It won't last long after I leave, I'm sure. You can s-say I trapped you and—"

He burst out laughing. "You don't know much about men, do you, honey? I'm not about to admit being trapped! But I wasn't talking about the gossip."

"You weren't? But what else is the problem?"

Though he smiled, he shook his head. "Emma, Emma, Emma. The problem is what happens now. You and Andy and I are linked together for life."

"No," she said, calm again. "We're not. Andy and I are moving away. We're not going to intrude in your life. So there's nothing to talk about."

"What if I don't want you to move away? What if I want to be a part of Andy's life?"

Those pesky tears came back, just when she thought she was under control. "Don't," she pleaded, her voice husky. She pulled her hand away from him.

He cleared his throat. "Yeah, well, I don't have any answers, but I thought if we played it day by day, maybe we'll come up with an answer. You need to stay here for a month, at least. And you're organizing my book collection while you're here. So we've got some time to work things out. Okay?"

"A month? I thought another week or two." She was sure that was what she'd agreed to.

He shook his head. "We'll see. Let's make an agreement. We'll work through each day's problems at breakfast the next morning."

"But that means you have to change your schedule!"

"Yeah," he agreed with a grin. "And I'm liking it. The crew has been complaining that I'm not spending enough time with you. So everyone's happy."

"Billy—"

"We can run him off for a while. He'll do anything to make sure you stay."

Emma couldn't think of anything to say. She started to tell him she couldn't stay. But he was right. She couldn't leave right away. Not and keep Andrea safe. So she'd wait, take it day by day.

He stood, then leaned down to kiss her cheek again, she supposed, but much to her horror, when she turned her head to see what he was doing, his lips landed on hers.

Ryan caught up with his manager and four other riders who were checking the herd in the lower pasture for new mamas and their babies and those cows who should deliver any moment.

"How's it going?" he asked Baxter as he rode up.

"Not bad. I decided to take a couple of the first-time mamas back to the barn. One of the boys found the tracks of a pack of wolves who've been through here since the last rain. What do you want to do?"

"Any calves missing?"

"Not yet."

"Hmm. Let's move them in closer. That pasture just north of the homeplace is ready to be used again. We can get them moved today if we start now."

"You going to help us, or do you have something else you need to do?" Baxter asked.

Ryan raised his eyebrows. "I'm here, aren't I?"

"Yeah. Oh, and boss?" Baxter paused before passing his orders on, "It's good to see you smiling." Then he rode off.

Ryan sat on his horse, watching his friend go about his business. It struck Ryan that he felt lighter, more involved, than he had for the past couple of years. Even when he'd spent time with Emma last fall, he'd been fighting what he was doing, feeling more guilty than ever because he was enjoying what he was doing.

Now, he had a reason for Emma being in his life. Merilee would never expect him to ignore his child. And those little caresses he'd been giving Emma were just so she'd feel wanted.

Yeah, right. Honesty forced him to admit that those touches brought him pleasure, too. Maybe more than they did to Emma.

When he'd accidentally kissed her on the mouth this morning, she'd jerked back, looking horrified. A good thing, too, because Ryan's inclination was to kiss her again. A real kiss this time.

Now that his parents had forced him to face the future, he could admit that he'd never intended Emma and Andy to leave. To go out into the world, unprotected, alone.

You didn't do such a good job last time protecting your loved ones. A year ago, that thought would've devastated him. But now, he admitted he had done nothing wrong. That day, he'd taken the morning off from the ranch work to go with his wife and son. The sheriff had told him nothing could've been done to change the outcome.

Finally, he was accepting the truth. Was it because so much time had passed? Or was it because he'd found Emma? Not that he loved her as he had Merilee. Or that Andy could replace Ryan, Jr. But she needed him. Andy needed him.

And that felt good.

And that kiss this morning told him he still wanted Emma. They were good together in bed. They could make a go of a life together. He'd be a good husband.

The relief flowing through him was incredible. Relief that he'd worked out a way to keep the two of them close. They wouldn't be his real family, but he'd be doing the right thing.

Having settled everything in his mind, he felt even better. He urged his horse forward, ready to work with more enthusiasm than he'd felt in ages.

Only one little question remained, one trouble-some question. Would Emma agree?

That sweet kiss stayed in Emma's mind all day.

And told her a month wasn't a possibility.

She pushed herself to work hard. She began clean-ing the dishes until Billy returned to the kitchen and reprimanded her.

She explained about her arrangement with Ryan to organize the books his grandfather left him. When Billy protested against her doing any work, she as-sured him she just wanted to do some reading, some thinking about the project. But she needed to see the books before she could do any of that.

Reluctantly, Billy led her upstairs to a back room filled with cartons of books.

"Oh, my!" she exclaimed. She hadn't been cer-tain that Ryan was telling the truth. But he had been. There was a lot to be done.

"Could you carry a couple of the boxes downstairs so I can go through them, please, Billy?"

"If you promise not to overwork," he agreed with a frown.

"No, I won't. Though I need to get better. I can't have you waiting on me all the time."

"Don't see why not. That's what I'm here for."

She smiled and pointed out a couple of boxes. Not that it mattered which ones. She just picked the two closest ones.

"Do you have any idea what room he's thinking about using for a library?" She hadn't really gone through the house, checking out the various rooms.

"Don't know, but I'd suggest the living room. No one uses that room. Everybody always comes in the back door, you know, and either sits down in the kitchen or the den."

"That's good thinking, Billy. Then let's put the boxes in the living room. They'll be out of everyone's way."

In a few minutes, she was settled in the room. Billy offered to dust everything before she started work, apologizing for not having done so already, but she sent him away. "Don't be silly. You do more work than anyone I've seen. I can dust a little if it bothers me."

"I'll call you for lunch," he said. "Don't work too hard."

"No, I won't," she promised again.

When he'd finally left her alone, she sighed and leaned down to open the first box.

But her choice didn't hold library books. It held photo albums. Emma knew she should close the box and not go through it, but photo albums weren't things she'd ever had. She had a few pictures from one foster family. She'd lived with them for two years. Then her foster mother had gotten ill and they'd had to take Emma away.

She couldn't imagine having an entire history of family life hidden away. With a quick look at the door, to be sure no one was watching, she lifted an album out of the box and opened it.

Andy called Emma before Billy did. The baby was on a four-hour feeding schedule. Emma hurriedly washed her hands to remove the dust and rushed to the nursery. She was tired…and sad. She was ready for a break.

She and Billy got to the nursery at the same time.

"How's the little darlin'?" he asked, peeping past Emma.

"I'd guess she's mad," Emma said. "Are all babies this impatient?"

"If Ryan's the daddy, they are. Why, Ryan, Jr.…." he broke off, looking horrified. "Sorry, I didn't mean—"

"Does Ryan never talk about his son or his wife?" she asked softly.

Billy looked grim. "Nope. He told me he didn't want me to say anything about 'em."

Emma sighed. She'd suspected as much. Which told her, as if she hadn't already figured it out, that Ryan would hate her looking at the pictures. He would hate her putting the loose pictures in the half-empty album that had pictures of his family.

"I don't mind if you talk about them, Billy. It must've been nearly as hard on you as it was on Ryan."

"It was hard," Billy admitted, "but Ryan almost lost his mind. I was so busy trying to take care of him, I got through it easier. He didn't have anything to pull him out of his despair. Until you come along."

Emma gave a half-hearted smile. She had already figured out, after she heard about Ryan's loss, that she'd been a distraction, and a physical release for Ryan. Nothing more.

"Well, I'd better feed this impatient little lady," Emma said. She'd been changing her diaper while they talked. She sat down in the rocker while Billy returned to the kitchen.

Though she heard the phone ring while Andy was sucking, she didn't worry about answering it. Billy was around. Besides, she wasn't a member of the family. She burped Andy until she responded with a loud belch.

"You must've gotten that from your daddy, too, little girl," Emma whispered to her baby as she snuggled her to her chest.

"Emma?" Billy called, giving her a chance to arrange her clothing before he entered.

"Yes, come in, Billy."

"Do you mind waiting a few minutes for lunch?"

"Of course not," she responded as he came into view. "If lunch is too much trouble, I can—"

"No, but Leigh and Beth want to come over and join us, so I need to fix some more. You don't mind, do you?"

"That they come visit? Of course not. It's not my place to—"

"'Course it is. They're coming to see you and the little princess, there. I told them you might be tired 'cause you've been working all morning. They said you could take a nap after lunch." He was staring at her, as if trying to judge her energy level.

"I've been sitting down, Billy. I'm fine." She tried to remember whether she'd put everything away in the living room. She didn't think she had since Andy had been crying. But Billy had said no one went in there. She hoped not. She'd be mortified if anyone found out she'd been snooping.

Andy didn't seem eager to go back to sleep, so Emma followed Billy to the kitchen, carrying her baby. "I'll sit down and watch if you don't mind, Billy. Maybe I'll pick up some new recipes for later."

Billy stopped what he was doing and whirled around. "Later?"

Emma shrugged her shoulders, trying to think of a simple answer that wouldn't upset the man. "You know, when I need a recipe for a church social or something."

"Next one that comes along, I'll help you make something special," he said and returned to his cooking.

Emma breathed a sigh of relief. It was hard enough to talk to Ryan about the future. She didn't want to have to do so with Billy, too.

After a few minutes of peace, in which she talked to Andy, encouraging her to coo, which immediately drew Billy to look over her shoulder, slowing down the cooking, they both heard a car.

"There they are. Perfect timing."

"I didn't slow you down too much?" she asked.

"Naw. Though the princess is a distraction."

The back door opened as someone called, "Hello?" Beth and Leigh came in.

"Oh, there you are!" Leigh exclaimed and hurried to Emma's side, her hands held out to take Andy.

Emma surrendered her baby, but since Leigh sat

down next to her, she didn't go too far. Beth, with
Jackson in her arms, sat on Emma's other side.

"How are you, Beth? How's Jackson?" Emma
asked.

"We're fine. Mom's taking good care of me.
Which is a good thing, because Jack's got a new case
and he can scarcely take his mind off it."

"Now, Beth, you know he has to support the two
of you," Leigh said gently. "After a man has his
first child, he feels a new responsibility."

"I know, Mom, but I miss him."

Emma was amazed that Beth was actually pouting.
She'd always seemed so levelheaded.

"I'm sure he's paying you more attention than
Ryan is Emma, and she's not complaining."

"Yeah, but she's not his wife and Andy's not his
first baby!" Beth snapped, obviously irritated by her
mother's comparison. Then she slapped her hand
over her lips in horror. "Oh, Emma, I'm sorry! I
didn't think—"

"No, you certainly didn't!" her mother snapped
in return.

"Please, Mrs. Nix, Beth, it's all right. You didn't
say anything that wasn't true," Emma assured them.

"Yes, but she didn't have to throw it in your
face," Leigh Nix complained, not satisfied.

Beth's eyes filled with tears. "I didn't mean to
hurt you, Emma."

Emma reached over for Beth's baby. "You didn't.
Let me see Jackson. He's so much bigger than
Andy." Emma took the baby and began asking

questions about how he was doing. Beth grew distracted, bragging about her son.

Then Billy served lunch and joined them at the table, and the conversation turned general.

Emma was enjoying all the company. She'd lived such a lonely life during her pregnancy, she found pleasure in talking to the other women.

Until Leigh asked about her work. "I think it's wonderful that you're taking care of all those books, but we don't want you getting too tired."

"Oh, no! I'm—I'm not doing much. Just checking out what's there."

"My father was quite a reader. Not much of a rancher, but he read everything he could get his hands on. He read to us kids, too, on winter nights when it got dark early. We didn't watch much television. Of course, that was a different time period."

"Yeah, but I can still remember Grandpa reading to me and Ryan," Beth added. She looked at Emma. "We loved it. Grandpa had this awesome voice and he'd act out the parts."

"How wonderful," Emma exclaimed, adding reading out loud to her mental list of what she'd do for Andy.

"Did you have—" Beth began, but Leigh interrupted her.

"Child, you're not letting Emma enjoy her lunch. Take Jackson from her so she can eat."

Both young women protested.

"Actually, he's going to sleep," Emma said. "Do you want me to put him in the nursery?"

"But Andy's asleep, too," Beth pointed out. "She'll need her crib."

"Ryan bought a bassinet and a crib, so we have plenty of room." Emma pushed away from the table, ready to carry Jackson from the table, but Billy leaped up and rushed to her side.

"I can put the little fella in his bed," he said. "Just give him to me."

"And I'll take care of Andy. You two need to eat more," Leigh ordered as she followed Billy out of the kitchen.

Beth laughed. "I love everyone telling me to eat more. It's the first time in ages I haven't had to worry about gaining weight."

Emma smiled. "I'd never know it. You always look so wonderful."

"And that's why I like you, friend," Beth said with a grin. "You lie like a trouper!"

They were both chuckling when Billy and Leigh came back in and sat down.

Emma relaxed, thinking how nice the luncheon had been.

"You know, Emma," Leigh said as she finished eating, "as soon as lunch is over, I'd love to look at some of my father's books. Do you mind?"

Emma froze. She hadn't been looking at books. She'd been going through the family's personal photo albums. And now Leigh and Beth would know that.

Chapter Nine

Ryan swung down from the saddle with a sigh of satisfaction. A good day's work in a place he loved. Coming home to his family.

He hadn't felt this way since before the accident. An elixir that said all's right with the world. They should bottle it and relieve the world of its problems.

"We'll take care of your horse, boss. Go on in," one of his hands said.

As tempting as that offer was, because he was anxious to see Emma and Andy, Ryan refused. "Thanks, but I'll take care of old Gus. He took care of me today."

When all the chores had been completed, he said goodnight and headed for the house. He had definite plans for the evening. He was going to explain to Emma the future he'd planned for the two—no, three of them.

Before he even got to the house, he had an inkling

his plans would fall apart…or at least be delayed. His sister's car was parked by the house. He guessed his mother and Beth had come for a visit.

But they'd have to go home and prepare dinner for the menfolk, so everything would fall into place. Unless they'd worn Emma out. She pushed herself too hard.

He picked up speed, his long strides bringing him to the back porch just as he heard another vehicle. Frowning, he took a step back and saw his father and Jack get out of the car. Guests for the evening weren't in his plans.

"Hey, Ryan!" his father called with a big smile, walking toward him.

"Hi, Dad, Jack. What are you doing here?"

Joe raised his eyebrows, then leaned toward Jack. "That doesn't sound too welcoming, does it?"

"Of course you're welcome, Dad," Ryan hurriedly said. 'I didn't know you were coming, though, did I?"

"Nope. You got plans?"

Ryan guessed he didn't. "No, of course not. I'm just coming in from work. I'll need to shower before I entertain guests. Unlike Jack, I don't handle clean-smelling paper all day."

Jack spoke for the first time. "You have an elevated idea of a lawyer's work, Ryan. Some of that paper stinks. At least what's written on it does."

They'd moved to the porch while they were talking and Ryan held open the door. "Come on in."

Billy and Leigh were in the kitchen, bustling around. Leigh spun around when she heard them, dropped the spoon she'd been using in the sink and rushed to hug her husband.

Ryan backed away when she approached him. "I've got to clean up, Mom."

"Well, hurry up. Dinner will be ready in half an hour." She hugged Jack and returned to the stove.

"Where's Emma?" he asked, not moving.

"And Beth?" Jack added, looking a little lost.

"Oh, I insisted they both lie down and rest while the babies were sleeping. We'll wake them up in a few minutes."

"Uh, I'll go wake Beth now," Jack said, backing toward the door. "Which room is she in?"

Ryan stood there, jealousy consuming him. Until he and Emma had had their talk, he knew she'd protest if he joined her in her bedroom.

After Leigh told Jack where to find his wife, he disappeared.

"Ryan? Aren't you going to shower?"

"Uh, yeah, I'll hurry."

"You've got half an hour," Leigh called.

But he stopped hurrying when the door closed behind him.

Instead of heading for the stairs, he looked down the hall to where Emma and Andrea had their rooms. He took a step in that direction, then halted again.

Damn, he smelled like a horse. Even Andy wouldn't want him the way he was. Later, when she was older, maybe two or three, he'd teach her about horses. He grinned, picturing his little girl sitting on a horse, holding on for dear life, while he led the horse around the corral. They had pictures of Beth like that.

Fed by that vision of the future, he turned and took the stairs two at a time. After he cleaned up, he'd check on Andy, even if he couldn't check on Emma, which he most wanted to do.

When he came down fifteen minutes later, he headed for Andy's room, but he found it empty. Stepping across the hall, he put his ear against the door. Emma's soft voice, talking to her baby, confirmed his guess. Andy was having dinner.

He remembered the nights in Emma's bed, that same voice wrapping around him, filling him. Her low, musical tones wove a magic that seduced him as much as her body.

And would do so again. Just as soon as he told her his decision. Oh, they couldn't have sex for a while. He remembered after Merilee gave birth. She'd not only wanted more time, she'd demanded he wait on her hand and foot before she let him back into her bed.

He grinned now, but at the time, he'd been a little miffed. But Emma was generous. She reached out— as she had last fall. Andy was a lucky little girl to have Emma for a mama.

The kitchen door swung open and his father stuck his head into the hall and yelled, "Ryan? Dinner's ready!"

Ryan jumped a foot, hoping to disguise what he'd been doing. "Uh, I'm here, Dad. I was checking on Andy."

His father looked at the closed door beside Ryan.

"Uh-huh. We heard Andy, and your mother went to check on her. Emma said they'd be in as soon as she fed her."

"Oh. Uh, okay, I'm coming." Like he had a choice. It was embarrassing to be discovered hanging around a closed door, like a bird waiting for a worm to come out of its hole.

Beth, with Jackson in her arms, had joined his family, Ryan noted when he reached the kitchen. He greeted his sister and touched Jackson's head. He was a handsome boy, but Andy was beautiful, he thought with pride.

"Is Emma ready yet?" Leigh asked as she carried a platter of steak over to the table.

"I don't think so. I didn't want to disturb her so I didn't knock."

"I'll check on her. Oh, Ryan, we have a lovely surprise for after dinner." Then she left the kitchen.

Ryan frowned. "What's she talking about, Billy? A new dessert?"

Billy didn't look at him, pretending to be too busy at the oven. "Uh, no."

His cook was a good man, straightforward. What was going on?

"Beth, what's Mom talking about?" he asked.

"I'm not telling. If I did, it wouldn't be a surprise." She didn't look at him either, keeping her gaze fixed on her son.

Was he overreacting? Could Billy be too busy to face him? Did Jackson demand his mother's attention? He heard footsteps coming back down the hall.

When his mother entered, Emma, with Andrea in

her arms, was right behind her. Ryan hurried to her side, reaching out to touch his daughter. Her eyes were open and he'd swear Andy looked at him.

At least *someone* had, because Emma never looked up.

Ryan's appetite, usually large after being in the saddle all day, gradually disappeared. His mother was bright and chatty. Emma was completely silent.

Something was wrong. Had his mother hurt Emma's feelings? Was Emma going to run away again? What had happened?

He couldn't get any answers.

"Billy, could I have some more iced tea?" Emma asked. She was still holding Andy, in spite of his mother's offer to take her.

Billy jumped up from the table and hurried to the counter where a pitcher of tea waited.

Ryan took the opportunity to insist on taking Andy. "I'll hold her while you finish your dinner, Emma. I'm through."

She took a quick look at his plate. Then she looked at him for the first time since he'd come into the house. "You didn't eat much."

"I guess I'm too excited about Mom's surprise."

Emma's face paled, much as it had in the hospital, and she looked upset.

"Emma, what's wrong? Do you hurt somewhere? Should we call Steve?" Ryan demanded, bending toward her.

Without a word, a hand covering her mouth, Emma ran from the kitchen.

Ryan was stunned. But he jumped up to follow her, the baby still in his arms.

"Ryan, wait!" his mother ordered.

He spun around, staring at her. "Why? What's going on? Did you upset Emma?"

"She's—she's not upset. Not really. Everything's going to be fine."

"Mom," Beth said softly, "I don't think we should."

Leigh's jaw clenched. "I do. It's important."

Joe Nix stared at his wife. "What are you up to, Leigh? You're not interfering again, are you?"

"I'm doing what has to be done, Joe Nix!"

Ryan stood holding his child, trying to decide whether he should go after Emma first, or try to figure out what was going on, when the kitchen door opened again and Emma entered the kitchen.

"I—I came back to get Andy," she said with determination. "I'm finished eating, so—"

"So why don't you tell me why you're upset?" Ryan said, not handing his daughter over. "What has my mother done that upset you?"

Emma wanted to shrink to ant size, so she could scurry out of the kitchen without anyone noticing. In spite of her protests, the day was swiftly descending into hell. And it was all her fault.

She'd confessed to Leigh and Beth that she'd found the albums and had been looking at the family pictures. Instead of anger, she'd been met with enthusiasm. The two ladies were eager to look, too.

Emma had been relieved and gladly shared the treasure she'd found. Leigh and Beth had taken turns telling tales about their family. Even Ryan's wedding pictures, with the beautiful Merilee, and the early pictures of him and his wife, their precious little boy in their arms, were talked about.

Emma had showed Leigh the stacks of pictures made the last year before the accident and asked her if Ryan would mind if she filled the last album with them, so they wouldn't get damaged.

Leigh had thought it was a good idea, and the three of them had spent the afternoon doing it. Emma knew Ryan wouldn't appreciate her action now, but in later years perhaps he would. Family albums were such treasures.

Then Leigh had dropped her bombshell.

They would stay for dinner, with their husbands joining them, and they'd spend the evening looking at all the pictures.

Just thinking about Ryan's anger and heartsickness made Emma ill. She'd protested. She'd pleaded. But Leigh was adamant. Ryan had to face his past before he could build a future.

"It's unnatural to mourn anyone as long as Ryan has. Merilee was a good person, but she had her faults as much as anyone. Ryan has turned her into a saint."

Beth tried to intervene. "I know you're right, Mom, but are you sure tonight is a good night? Ryan's not going to like it."

"I think we should've faced the past before. We've let him hide. Tonight, we're going to talk about that sweet little boy and the happiness they shared."

Then she got up and headed for the kitchen to consult with Billy.

Emma had covered her face with her hands. "He's going to hate me even more than he does."

"Oh, Emma, he doesn't hate you. He couldn't!" Beth had exclaimed.

Emma took down her hands, her face tragic. She whispered, "He hates what I've done to him. He didn't want a new child, a new family."

Beth reached out to take Emma's hand. "Maybe he doesn't know what he wants? Maybe Mom's right?"

After hearing Beth's words, a tiny flame of hope had burned in Emma's heart all afternoon. But now Ryan hadn't even found out what was about to happen and he was angry. His mother had been wrong. Emma wanted to run away.

But not without her baby.

"I want Andy," she said, squaring her shoulders and looking at him.

"You can have her after you tell me what's wrong."

"You can't hold her hostage!" Emma protested.

Before Ryan could respond, his father stood. "Son, let Emma have her baby. Your mother is going to tell us what's going on. Aren't you, Leigh?"

Since his words sounded more like an order than a suggestion, Emma wasn't surprised when Leigh agreed.

"Of course, I'll be glad to tell you. Billy, let's clear off the table. We can have dessert later. Then

I'll show you the surprise.'' She paused and looked at Emma. ''I want you to stay, Emma, please?''

Emma nodded, feeling she had no choice. If she'd gone about her business, as she'd intended, and checked out the books, none of this would've happened. So she should be here, a target for Ryan's anger, because it was her fault.

Holding out her hands for Andrea, she tucked the baby on her shoulder and sat down.

Ryan knew something was wrong. He was getting a sick feeling in his gut that he didn't like at all. Emma was still pale, and he felt sure she'd lost her dinner a few minutes ago. Now, although she appeared composed, her face remained pale, and she refused to look at anyone.

All her attention was trained on Andy, who was almost ready to go to sleep.

Billy wiped the table down, then he and Leigh left the room with instructions for everyone to wait right there.

Ryan saw Jack and Beth whispering. Then Jack got an alarmed look on his face, and his gaze flew to Ryan before he quickly looked away. Ryan straightened his shoulders. Whatever was coming wouldn't be pleasant. He knew Jack, trusted his judgment. The fact that he thought this surprise was going to be a disaster worried Ryan.

The door swung open and Leigh entered to put three large albums on the table. Billy carried five.

''Today, Beth and Emma and I had a wonderful time going through the family albums. I thought it would be fun for the rest of you to share, too. Do you remember when you fell in that mud puddle, Ryan, and I got my camera and took a picture? It's so funny!''

Ryan sat, frozen, unable to believe his mother was doing this to him. Everyone was watching. Emma was sitting beside him, holding his child. His second child. And his mother wanted him to look at pictures of his first child and his beloved wife.

That was the point of this exercise.

He stood.

''No!'' he protested harshly, his voice rough with emotion. ''I can't do this.''

''Joe?'' Leigh pleaded to her husband, even as she blocked the door out of the kitchen.

His father stared at his wife. Then he shifted his gaze to his son. Ryan saw the love and concern in his father's eyes. His parents had been wonderful when the accident had occurred. They'd stayed with him, helped him through the agony. He respected his parents.

But he couldn't do this.

''Son, I think your mother has a point. You've hidden from life for too long.''

Betrayal flooded him. He couldn't believe his father thought this torture was a good idea. ''No! You can't expect me to—to—''

''To go on living?'' Joe said softly, staring at him. ''You've sacrificed too many years already. Now you've got a chance for a new life.''

''No!'' Ryan shouted again, each time his voice louder, more stressed. ''I can't relive that agony. I can't—I can't do this!'' Though he felt like a coward, he knew his limitations. Rather than face his mother, he turned and charged through the back door, out of the house.

Emma sat at the table, her head bowed, tears streaming down her cheeks.

She'd known he would be hurt. And she'd let it happen. Had caused it to happen. He would never forgive her.

But then, he would never forgive her for Andy, either. She hugged her baby tighter against her. He might regret their child's birth. But she didn't and never would.

She shoved away from the table and headed for the door. But Leigh was still there and put her hands on Emma's shoulders.

''Emma, darling, don't cry. Please don't cry,'' Leigh pleaded, hugging her close.

Emma had never expected to feel a mother's touch from Leigh Nix. But that was exactly what she'd gotten. It shocked her. She looked at the woman, gratitude mixed with sorrow. ''I'm so sorry,'' she murmured.

Joe Nix came around the table and heard her words. ''What do you have to be sorry for, Emma?''

''It's my fault. I shouldn't have looked at the albums, but—but I've never had—without a family there isn't much need of albums. I-If I hadn't been looking at them, this—'' she waved one hand toward the table ''—wouldn't have happened. Ryan wouldn't be angry.''

Joe took her from Leigh's embrace and wrapped his big burly arms around her. "None of this is your fault. You didn't do anything bad. You've given us a beautiful granddaughter, and you've shared her with us."

Emma sniffed against his chest. She wished she could feel those protective arms forever. It must be how a child feels when her father consoles her. With him on her side, she knows she can take on the world. A feeling Andy would never have.

She couldn't indulge herself for long. She'd grow too weak. Backing out of his embrace, she said, "I— I have to go. Ryan won't want me here when he comes back."

Everyone in the room protested, but Emma couldn't face Ryan again.

Shaking her head, hugging Andrea tightly, she didn't try to argue with them. She hurried to her room.

Ryan stood at the corral, his arms resting on the top rail, his head bent in sadness. How could his family be so cruel? They'd supported him when Merilee and Ryan, Jr., had died. Why had they turned on him now?

"Feeling sorry for yourself?" his father asked quietly.

Ryan spun around, almost losing his balance. "You haven't tortured me enough?" he shouted.

His father strolled over to the corral and leaned against it beside him. "Yeah, looking at pictures is the last word in torture these days."

"You're making fun of me now? Better you take a knife and stab me. Let me die!"

"Okay," his father calmly agreed and Ryan stared at him. What was wrong with his father tonight? Had he gone crazy?

"And we'll keep a close eye on Emma and Andy. 'Course, we'll be going back to Florida in a few days, but we'll send them Christmas presents and birthday cards each year. That'll probably make them feel okay."

Ryan's heart clutched. He hadn't been thinking about Emma or Andy. He admitted he'd only been thinking of himself. Of his loss. Of his pain.

"I'll take care of them," he said stonily, his face wiped clean of emotion. He wasn't going to tell his father again how much he was hurting him.

"Might be hard to do," his father said, shrugging. "Seems Emma blames herself for what happened tonight and she's inside packing."

Chapter Ten

Ryan whirled around, ready to charge to the house and stop Emma's departure. This time he'd nip her disappearing act in the bud. She was being ridiculous.

His father caught him by the arm, pulling him to a halt. "Where are you going?"

"I'm going to stop Emma. She's not ready to be out on her own. Anybody can see that!" he snapped.

"So you're going to march in there and tell her she can't go?"

"That's right."

"What gives you the right to keep her here?"

He didn't like his father's question. "I'm the father, remember?"

"So I've heard. But you're not the husband. Jack said you'll have to go to court to get visitation rights if Emma wants to be difficult."

"Emma wouldn't—it doesn't matter. We're going

to get married. I was going to tell her tonight. If you hadn't interfered, everything would be settled by now.'' He heard his so-there attitude in his voice and felt ashamed. ''I don't mean you weren't welcome, but I intend to do the responsible thing.''

His father put his hand on his shoulder. ''Son, we never doubted for a minute that you'd be responsible.''

That sentiment should've felt good, but something wasn't right. ''If you trusted me, what was tonight all about?'' he asked.

''It was about your being happy.''

''What are you talking about?''

''You've mourned Merilee's and the baby's deaths for a long time. That's understandable. It was a shocking loss. But you need to put it behind you if you're going to be happy.''

''I told you I'm going to marry her!'' Ryan snapped, tired of his father's words.

''When you proposed to Merilee, did you *tell* her what *she* was going to do?''

His father's question didn't make sense. ''Of course not! She had a mind of her own, and she wasn't above making me pay a price,'' he said, his mind going back to the night he proposed, a grin on his face.

''What makes you think Emma is any less deserving of a real proposal?''

''This is different!'' Ryan roared, not liking what he was hearing.

''How?''

"There's a baby involved, my baby. Emma shouldn't have to bear the responsibility by herself."

"I agree. I know you'll offer child support. But Emma seems to be independent. Probably because she hasn't had anyone to rely on in her life. I doubt she'll accept a demand to marry."

"She will. Family is important to Emma. She wants Andy to have the best. Of course she'll accept." His father's words were eroding his confidence. He had everything planned. Of course it would work out. He was sure of it. His father had to be wrong.

Like he always was?

His father was always right. It had irritated Ryan when he was a teenager, cocky, ready to conquer the world. Then he'd matured and appreciated his father's experience and wisdom.

But this time he was wrong. And Ryan was going to show him just how wrong he was. "She's going to be pleased. And I'm going to tell her right now." He shrugged off his father's hand and headed for the house.

Joe Nix stood there in the darkness, wryly grinning. He didn't think his son's approach was going to work, but for the first time in a long time, Joe hoped he was wrong.

Both Leigh and Beth tried to talk Emma out of leaving.

"I appreciate the support you've both given me, but I'm stronger, and I believe it's important that I get out of Ryan's life." Leigh started to object, but

Emma held up a hand to stop her. "I believe it's important to me and to Andy. I won't allow my daughter to be an also-ran in her father's heart."

"I'm sure he'd come to love her," Leigh said, anguish in her voice.

Emma tried to smile, but it was too hard. "We'll be fine. I'll take it easy for another week. That should be plenty of time. I have enough money saved to take care of that, especially since Ryan paid all my hospital bills."

She didn't have all that much to pack. Andy's things didn't take up a lot of room, and she'd mostly worn her robe and nightgowns since she arrived. Only today had she actually dressed. "I think that's all. If you don't think Ryan will mind, I'll take those disposable diapers with me."

"You take whatever you need," Leigh said, "and I'll be bringing you some food tomorrow, so I'll pick up some more diapers."

"Mrs. Nix, I don't want to cause any problems between you and Ryan. We'll be fine."

"Yes, you will, because I'm going to see to it. And call me Leigh."

"Are you sure you don't mind driving me to town?"

"Jack and I are going to drive you," Beth said. "Mom and Dad are going to take Jackson on home."

"Are you sure, Beth? You're not too tired?"

"I'm sure. I'm just sorry my brother is so blind he can't see what he's giving up."

Emma hugged her. "It's not Ryan's fault that he doesn't love us, Beth. Don't be angry with him."

The door to her room swung open and Ryan charged in. "Emma, you're not leaving."

Much to Emma's surprise, Leigh stepped between her son and Emma and said, "You have no say in the matter. You can't keep her here like a prisoner."

Ryan frowned ferociously at his mother. "She's not a prisoner. But there's no need for her to go. We're getting married."

Emma couldn't have been more stunned if he'd slapped her. Then tears gathered in her eyes. There was her dream on a big plate in front of her. All she had to do was say okay, and she'd have a family for her and Andy. A father for her child.

And she had to say no.

Because the offer had no substance. He didn't love them or want them. He wanted Merilee and Ryan, Jr.

"We'll get married as soon as you're ready," he continued. "I'm fine with next week, but if you want to wait until we can have a big wedding, that's okay, too."

"No," she said softly, and picked up the one bag she'd packed.

"Don't carry that, Emma. Jack will get it," Beth urged.

"What do you mean, no?" Ryan questioned at the same time, anger filling him.

"I can't marry you, Ryan, but thank you for asking. Beth, would you call Jack, then? I'm ready to go as soon as I get Andy from her crib."

Ryan blocked the doorway. "I thought marriage

is what you wanted? We'll be a family. You said you wanted a family.''

Emma's tears dried up. She was faced with a hard-headed man unwilling to be honest with either her or himself. If she didn't make things clear tonight, she'd have him on her doorstep in the morning. She wanted to end the emotional roller coaster now.

"Why are you offering to marry me, Ryan?"

"That's a dumb question. We have a child,'' he snapped.

Beth moaned, and Emma wanted to. It was a good thing she'd realized how Ryan felt. "A marriage is more than a responsibility. I don't intend to hide Andy from you. But I won't make a loveless marriage for her either. I knew you didn't want her. I didn't tell you about her early on because I was afraid you'd insist on an abortion.''

Everyone gasped except Emma.

"When I made that decision, I knew that meant I had to be responsible for my child. I promise you Andy will be happy. You don't have to worry.''

She tried to walk past him, but he blocked her way, taking her by the arms. "You're being ridiculous, Emma. We can make this work. Just because I love—was married before doesn't mean I can't re-marry.''

Emma stared at the handsome, *good* man standing before her. She loved him so much. But he felt nothing for her, and that kind of marriage wouldn't work.

"I hope you will remarry one day, Ryan, when you find someone you can love. But until then, I wouldn't advise it. Now, if you'll excuse me, I'm tired.''

The look of disbelief on his face made her want to hold him close, to assure him she'd do whatever he wanted. But she couldn't. She might be alone in the world, but she'd learned how to take care of herself. And she'd do the same for Andy. They'd be fine.

"Ryan," his mother prompted.

He stared blindly at her, as if he had no idea who she was. Emma took the opportunity to slip past him to the room across the hall. Andy was sleeping, wrapped in a little pink blanket. She lifted her daughter and wrapped a bigger blanket around her. Then she picked up the diaper bag and turned around.

Ryan was standing in the doorway watching her. "Don't take her away," he said hoarsely, softly.

"I have to," she told him, her voice gentle. "She can't grow up competing with a ghost. She's not your son. But she's a beautiful baby, my baby, and I want her to know that.''

"She's my baby, too!"

"Only if you want her to be. You have to decide that, Ryan, but I won't keep her from you. If you want to see her, you know where I live." For right now. She knew she'd have to move away as soon as she could manage, or she'd suffer too much heartache.

She pushed past him, and Leigh took the diaper bag from her. Beth had gone to the kitchen to summon Jack and they were coming out of Emma's bedroom.

"Ready?" Beth whispered, her gaze darting between Emma and her brother.

Emma nodded and hurried to the kitchen. There she made a tearful goodbye to Billy and Ryan's father, who'd come back into the house.

"Anything you need, Emma, let me know," Joe said, and Emma blinked back the tears.

"Thank you, but we'll be fine."

Then she hurried outside, leaving behind the only man she'd ever loved.

From a full house, suddenly Ryan was standing in an empty one. Billy was still there, but he was silent. Even if his family had remained, he realized, with sudden clarity, it would still be empty without Emma and Andy.

What was he going to do?

"You want some of that dessert your mama fixed?" Billy asked, his back to him, his voice gruff.

Ryan stared at him as if he was crazy. "No, damn it, I don't want dessert. I said I'd marry her! Why was that a bad thing? It's what she wanted when she talked to me last October. So I agreed! And she walks out? She's crazy. Good riddance!"

Billy had been rinsing the dishes and loading the dishwasher. He never left the kitchen dirty before going to bed. But he spun around, glaring at Ryan. "I didn't know you could be so dumb!" he yelled. Then he walked out of the kitchen. Ryan heard his bedroom door slam a few seconds later.

Everyone blamed him because Emma'd left? Hell, it was her decision. He hadn't wanted her to go. He'd said he'd marry her, take care of her and Andy. And she'd thrown it back in his face.

His father's words replayed in his head. Okay, so he hadn't proposed, exactly. He'd said the words, but he hadn't held her in the moonlight. Or offered her a ring. But, damn it, the circumstances were different. They had a baby! Sweet little Andy needed someone to take care of her!

He began pacing the kitchen, going through the events of the evening. Trying to find a way to make his plans work. He thought about how happy he'd been when he'd ridden home. How sure he'd been that he'd found happiness again.

He'd been satisfied that Merilee would understand. That she and Ryan, Jr., would nod, knowing they'd still be first in his heart. But he had to do the responsible thing.

And if he married Emma, he couldn't refuse to share her bed. Merilee wouldn't expect that of him. He could make love to her, as he did last fall. After all, a man had his needs. And she would be his wife.

Why was she causing so much difficulty? Why was she ruining everything?

He found no answers, so he kept pacing.

When Billy entered the kitchen the next morning early, to finish his work from last night, he discovered Ryan still there, sitting with his head on the table, his eyes closed.

"You stay up all night?" he asked, still angry at his boss because of Emma and the baby, but loving him like a favorite nephew, as he always had.

Ryan snapped his head up and blinked furiously. "What time is it?" he growled.

"Half past five. You want breakfast?"

Ryan ran both hands through his hair, hoping to ease the pounding in his head. He'd had a plan last night, at some point. What was it?

Oh, yeah, he was going to see Emma and explain how silly she was being. He was going to propose marriage again. He hadn't explained it right. She probably thought he intended to treat her like a sister. But she was wrong.

He couldn't go yet. It was too early. "Uh, I'm going to go take a nap. Wake me at eight. I'll eat then." He sure wasn't going to explain his plan to Billy. He was on Emma's side, though Ryan had a hard time figuring out what that side was.

Besides, he was the boss. He could have breakfast at eight if that was what he wanted to do. "Call Baxter and tell him I won't be joining him today."

Baxter and the cowboys could work without him. The man was a good manager.

"Okay." Billy stood staring at him, and Ryan couldn't stand the accusation in his cook's eyes.

"I'm going upstairs," he said stiffly, with none of the easy camaraderie he and Billy used to share.

Billy didn't respond. But after the door had swung to behind Ryan, he stood there, his hands on his hips and shook his head sadly from side to side.

Emma didn't waken until Andy's eight o'clock feeding. Her baby was establishing a routine that made it easier to plan. Every four hours she wanted to eat.

When Emma had left the hospital, the nurses had warned that Andy might need to eat more often because she was so little. And at first she had demanded her mother every two hours. But in the week and a half since, the time had stretched out to four hours.

She rolled out of bed and hurried to the nursery. "Good morning, sweetie. Mom's here." Mom and no one else. She missed the knowledge that there was always someone around to help out. To reassure her. To call for help if she needed it.

She stiffened her shoulders, determined to live with her decision. "Ready for a diaper change?" She took care of that job, then scooped Andy up to her shoulder and settled in the rocking chair she'd found at a garage sale right after she'd found out she was pregnant.

Only after Andy was fed, burped and tucked back into bed did Emma manage to feed herself. A box of toaster pastries, half-empty, was in her pantry. She'd definitely have to shop today. For milk if nothing else.

She was munching on her sparse breakfast, sipping some caffeine-free hot tea, when someone knocked on her door. She didn't even have her robe on. At least she was sure her visitor was not Ryan, but she didn't want anyone to see her with her hair all a mess and only her nightgown on.

"Just a minute," she called and hurried to her bedroom. Slipping on the robe, she smoothed her hair and returned to the front door. "Who is it?"

"Leigh and Joe," Ryan's mother called.

Emma hurriedly unlocked the door and let them in. They both had their arms full of groceries.

"What are you—" she began, but Leigh, followed by Joe, went past her to the kitchen. When she followed them, Leigh was filling her pantry.

"You didn't need to bring me groceries," she protested, embarrassed by their generosity.

"I realized you probably didn't have any milk, Emma, and I guess I got carried away," Leigh said with a disarming smile. "Joe always complains about my shopping."

"How are you, Emma?" Joe asked, smiling at her.

"I'm fine. Andy's in her crib, but I think she's still awake if you want to see her."

"Oh, Joe, go get her and bring her in here while I fix breakfast," Leigh said. Then she looked at Emma. "If you don't mind?"

"I don't mind you seeing Andy, but I just fixed my breakfast."

Leigh leaned around her and looked at the small table in the next room. "That's not enough breakfast when you're nursing a baby, dear. Besides, Joe and I haven't eaten either. You go sit down and I'll whip something up."

Joe came back in, holding Andy, a beaming smile on his face. "She sure is a good baby," he said, tilting his arms so his wife could see Andy's little face.

Emma couldn't help smiling. She loved compliments about Andy.

"You and Emma go sit down, Joe. She shouldn't

be standing around.'' Leigh opened a package of eggs and took down a mixing bowl.

"Come on, Emma," Joe said. "We'll sit at the table and you can finish your tea while we wait for breakfast.''

"Yes," Leigh agreed, but she set the mixing bowl on the counter and dashed to the table to take Emma's plate. "I'll just throw these nasty things out, though.''

Emma opened her mouth to protest, but Joe shook his head. "Taking care of you makes her feel better, Emma, if you don't mind.''

"Of course I don't mind, but it's not necessary. Coming back here was my decision." She didn't want them feeling guilty about her and Andy, any more than she wanted Ryan to feel "responsible.''

But since she couldn't deny Leigh this morning, she sat down, realizing she was already tired. Maybe because she hadn't slept well last night. Ryan wasn't the only one with something to mourn.

"That was a wonderful breakfast, Leigh, and I thank you and Joe for the groceries," Emma said after they'd lingered over a big breakfast, "but the two of you mustn't feel sorry for me, or think that you have to take care of me. Andy and I will be fine.''

"Of course you will be," Leigh agreed, "but I intend to be part of my grandchild's life, if you'll let me, Emma. And I consider you to be my daughter.''

Emma blinked rapidly. Darn, she'd promised herself she'd be strong. "I don't want to cause any problems between you and Ryan. I'd never keep you from Andy. But I think—"

Joe interrupted. "Emma, we love our son. That doesn't mean we think he's made the right decision. Unfortunately, he has to fight his way through this. Until he does, we intend to make sure you're okay."

Emma swallowed a lump in her throat. "Don't convince yourself he'll change his mind," she said softly. "He doesn't love me, and that's not his fault. If anything, it's all my fault because I—I slept with him before I realized how he felt."

Joe stood and began gathering the dirty dishes. "We'll play it by ear. In the meantime, you go get in bed and rest while we clean up."

"Don't you dare protest," Leigh added. "I haven't seen Joe volunteer for dish duty in a long time. I'm going to enjoy this!"

After those words, Emma had no choice. With a thanks, she rose to go back to her bedroom. A knock on the door stopped her.

"Beth? Surely she's not trying to help, too?" she said, looking at Joe and Leigh.

"Emma?" Ryan's voice came through the door.

All three of them froze. Then Joe set down the dishes he'd picked up.

"Want me to get it?" he asked.

Emma nodded, unable to speak.

Joe swung open the door.

Ryan stared at his father, then looked over Joe's shoulder to see Emma and his mother. "Damn it, what are you two doing here? Is this a conspiracy to make sure I don't get to talk to Emma alone?"

Chapter Eleven

Joe Nix ignored his son's protest and turned to Emma. "Do you want to invite him in or send him away?"

Emma bit her bottom lip to avoid smiling at Ryan's outraged expression. "He can come in. I told him he could see Andy."

"I'm not here to see Andy! I'm here to see you!"

Before Emma could respond, Leigh grabbed Joe's arm and said, "We'll be in the kitchen cleaning up, Emma. Call if you need us."

Since there was no door between the kitchen and the living area, there wouldn't be a lot of privacy, which was a good thing. One look at Ryan had her heart aching to comfort him. His eyes were bleary, his face drawn, as if he'd suffered.

"We can't talk here. Let's go to the bedroom," Ryan said, grabbing her hand and starting in that direction.

"No! We can talk quietly," she said, resisting. "Besides, we have nothing to talk about."

"Yes, we do. You misunderstood me yesterday. It took me a while to figure out what was wrong, but I finally did."

"You did? I thought I'd explained it."

"Yes, but I knew it had to be something, because I was offering you just what you asked for last October. That's why I was upset. Things weren't making sense to me. But now I understand."

Emma backed away from him. She was pretty sure she understood everything a lot more than Ryan did. And he wasn't going to be happy. "So explain it to me."

He shot a frustrated look toward the kitchen. They both could hear his parents talking as they cleaned.

"Damn it, Emma, I don't want them to overhear."

"If you talk quietly, they won't." She crossed her arms over her chest and waited.

"It's not like you thought. I didn't mean we'd live together like—like brother and sister." His face reddened but he kept his gaze on her.

Emma blinked several times, processing his words. He thought she—that thought had never entered her head. Even when he'd thrown her out, vowing never to see her again, she'd known he still wanted her. Their intimacy had been incredible. She knew that, even as inexperienced as she was, because of Ryan's reaction.

"We're good together," Ryan continued. "That part was never a problem. I mean, anyone can understand my having a—a relationship. I'm a man and men need—you know.''

"Sex?" she asked, just to irritate him.

"Sssh!" Ryan ordered, his gaze going nervously to the kitchen.

"Your parents know we had sex, Ryan. If we hadn't, Andy wouldn't have come along.''

"I know that!" he returned, his voice louder.

Emma saw his father look their way, but she smiled at him and he returned to drying the dishes.

"So, now that you understand, we can go ahead and get married,'' Ryan said, taking a step closer to her.

"No."

Her brief answer irritated him, but he stepped even closer.

"Don't try to tell me you didn't enjoy what we did, Emma Davenport!" he snapped.

Though she was embarrassed, she didn't hide from that fact. Raising her chin, she said, "No, I won't deny that. But then, I was in love with you."

"Was?" he asked with a frown.

He wanted his pound of flesh. Why not? It wasn't going to make any difference. "Okay, I *am* in love with you."

Smiling, he reached out for her. "Good. Then everything is all right."

"No."

"Stop saying that!" He paced several feet across the room and back. "Why isn't it okay?"

"It's not okay because you don't love me. You don't love Andy. I told you Andy can't compete with a ghost. Well, I have no intention of doing so, either. I've been alone all my life, Ryan. No one wanted me. But that doesn't mean I'll never be wanted. Someday I might find someone who can love me and love Andy. Until then, the two of us will be fine on our own.''

"You want me to say I love you?" he roared, his anger hot. "Okay, fine, I can say it. I love you, Emma. Please marry me! Is that what you want to hear?"

Emma stared at him. She was going to have to move away sooner than she'd thought. He was going to destroy her if she didn't. "No, that's what I want you to *feel*, Ryan. Not just say it to get your way."

"Damn you!" he muttered. Then, before Emma could respond, he seized her by the shoulders and kissed her. A hot, searing, desire-driven kiss that turned her knees to water.

When he released her, he turned around and stomped out of the apartment without saying good-bye.

Emma leaned against the wall, hoping she wouldn't fall forward on her face. Hunger raced through her body. Until Ryan had taught her, she'd thought all the talk about sex had been made up. But after two months of him holding her, making love to her, she'd believed in the magic of sharing love. Until he'd let her know the only love was on her part.

But she still wanted him.

"Are you okay, Emma?" Joe asked, touching her arm.

She hadn't even heard him approach. "Yes. Yes, I'm fine. Just a little tired."

"We're finished with the cleaning up," Leigh announced brightly, as if everything were normal. "Come lock the door behind us. Then promise you'll go straight to bed."

"Yes," she agreed. Her brain seemed to have been scrambled by Ryan's kiss. She couldn't think of much else to say.

When she fell into her bed after they left, a few tears escaped her tightly closed eyes. But she wasn't going to indulge in a sob fest. She'd made her choice.

She only hoped Ryan would accept it.

Billy was serving dinner at 8:00 p.m. a week later, when Ryan came in from work. For the past seven days, Ryan had been driving himself for long hours, working hard, coming in late. When he got there, he scarcely ate anything.

Billy was growing concerned that his boss would fall sick before he figured things out. He'd lost a lot of weight, his eyes, with circles beneath, seemed sunken, and his jeans didn't fit tight anymore.

"You gonna eat tonight, or just stir your food around like you've been doing lately?" he asked.

Ryan glared at him and took a bite of the roast.

Billy sat down beside him and served himself. "Baxter came to see me today."

Ryan's head reared up. "Is there a problem?"

"Yeah. And the problem is you. He's worried about you."

"That's ridiculous!"

"So are the hands. They're wondering what kind of disease you have and if it's contagious."

Ryan choked on his bite of food and had a coughing attack. "I'll set them straight," he muttered after he'd managed to stop the coughing.

"I doubt it."

Ryan glared again.

"Hell, boss, you're lookin' like you did after the accident, like you'd rather be dead than alive. The dogs are getting fat eatin' your dinners. Neither of those things is healthy."

"I'm all right," Ryan muttered, throwing down his fork.

"You gotta eat more than that," Billy protested and Ryan picked up his fork again.

They sat in silence, Ryan taking an occasional bite, staring into the distance.

"Talked to Leigh this morning. Beth and Emma are going in for their checkups tomorrow."

Ryan snapped his gaze to Billy. "Why?"

"Ladies go to the doctor after three weeks. Then they go again at six weeks, to see if everything's all right."

"She's not having any problems, is she?" Ryan demanded, leaning forward.

"I think Beth is doing fine," Billy assured him, an innocent look on his face.

"Damn it, you know I meant Emma!"

Satisfaction in Billy's eyes told Ryan he'd fallen into the old man's trap.

"I guess she's okay." There was a taste of doubt

in the words. "She didn't have as easy a time as Beth, you know."

"Of course I know! What time tomorrow?"

"Your mama didn't say." Billy was watching him.

Ryan took another bite to distract him.

"But she did say Andy is growing. And as cute as a button!" Billy added with a chuckle.

"What else would you expect her to say?" Ryan mumbled, but his heart ached. He hadn't seen or spoken to Emma or his child since he'd kissed her. To show her what she was missing, he assured himself.

Instead, all he'd done was torture himself. He couldn't sleep anymore, thinking about Emma, wanting her beside him. Wanting to hold Andy, to see for himself that she was growing.

Over and over again, he told himself all he had to do was say he loved her...and mean it. Tell her he no longer thought of Merilee as his wife. He no longer mourned for Ryan, Jr.

He hung his head, closing his eyes.

"Hey, boy, you're not falling asleep, are you? I'd hate for you to bury your face in my special roast beef."

"No. I was thinking." The same thing he'd been thinking over and over again. All day. All night. He pushed himself in the saddle, hoping to be tired enough to sleep when he got home, but so far it wasn't working.

He shoved back his chair and got up.

"Hey, you haven't eaten enough. You got to eat more!" Billy protested.

But Ryan was already at the door. "Not tonight," he said wearily.

He tromped down the hall to the small office he used. Falling into the chair, he picked up the phone and called Steve.

"Lambert here," Steve answered the phone.

"Steve, it's Ryan."

"Hey, Ryan, how's it going?"

"Fine. Want to meet at the café for dinner tomorrow night?"

"Sure. What's up?"

"Nothing much. Billy's tired of my company. I thought I'd give him a break and eat out."

"Good thinking. I should be finished about six. What's good for you?"

"How about six-thirty? That will give you a little extra time in case you have an emergency."

"Sounds good. I'll see you tomorrow evening, then."

Ryan slid into the booth and took the menu from the waitress. Not that he needed it. He'd eaten here a lot, although not since he'd broken up with Emma last October. Too many memories.

He scanned the menu to be sure there hadn't been any changes. Then he closed it and stared at the door, watching for Steve.

Leigh would've told him what he wanted to know, but he wasn't going to ask his mother. He didn't want Emma to know he was interested in her health. He wouldn't give her that satisfaction.

He pictured Emma in his head, her delicate features, dark hair, that beautiful smile. When he'd first met her, he'd thought her plain. Until she smiled.

Then they'd gone to dinner, and he'd thought she was beautiful in a quiet way. Now she was all he could think about.

Because she was his responsibility, he assured himself.

Before he could admit his lie, he caught sight of Steve and waved.

"Sorry I'm late," the doctor apologized as he slid into the booth across from Ryan.

"No problem. You know what you want to eat? I'll call Patti over."

"Sure, unless they've changed the menu," Steve said with a grin.

After they'd ordered, Ryan looked at Steve to find him staring back.

"Are you all right?"

"Don't you start, too," Ryan protested. "Billy's been on my back all week."

"You're beginning to look like skin and bones. Is anything wrong? Do you need to come see me?"

"Hell, no! I'm off my feed a little, not sleeping well. That's all. It'll go away."

The waitress brought out their salads and Ryan hoped food would distract Steve.

"Busy day, today?" he asked, trying to sound casual.

"No more than usual. How's the cow business? Having a lot of babies?"

Ryan's head snapped up.

"Calves, I mean. Uh, are you having a good crop? I heard the vet's been pretty busy."

"'Bout average."

They both ate some salad.

Ryan tried to think of a normal topic of conversation. "Heard Baily got kicked by that bull of his."

"Yeah. He insists on treating that miserable animal like a pet, but he's a mean son-of-a-gun."

"Heard he got an offer last month for him, an outrageous amount."

"He should've taken it. That bull would be hamburger meat before I'd let him attack me again." Steve grinned, but Ryan could feel his gaze traveling over Ryan, as if trying to judge his health.

"How's Beth?" Ryan asked, giving up on conversation. "Heard she was in today for her checkup."

"She's fine."

"And Emma?"

Steve stared at him before saying, "Fine."

"That doesn't tell me much."

Laying down his fork, Steve said, "Ryan, I'm not supposed to discuss my patients with anyone. You know that."

"I just want to know if she's all right. That's not exactly a detailed report."

"I told you she was fine."

The waitress brought their steaks and Ryan shoved the bowl of salad away. "You can take that."

After she'd gone, Steve said, "You didn't eat much salad. Green stuff is good for you."

"Yeah," Ryan muttered. "Is Emma eating properly?"

"Must be eating better than you. *She* doesn't look like a ghost."

"And Andy? Did you check Andy too?"

"Yeah. You've got a pretty little girl there. She didn't even cry, which is more than I can say for your nephew. That boy has healthy lungs."

"Has she gained any weight?"

"Yeah, she's almost half a pound over her birth weight."

"So Emma's not havin' any trouble, you know, feeding her?"

"No, she's not. Want me just to send you the file?"

Ryan started nodding before he realized Steve was teasing. "Hey, that's not nice!"

"Eat your steak."

Since Steve was following his own advice, Ryan picked up a knife and fork and toyed with the meat. But he had no appetite. All he could think about was his family.

Steve watched his friend while he enjoyed his own steak, and took note of the fact that Ryan wasn't eating at all. Which, of course, explained his hollow cheeks, his paleness. If he didn't miss his guess, Ryan had lost about ten pounds since the last time he'd seen him.

It was time to bring in the heavy artillery.

Jack and Joe sat in the den of Jack's house that same night, watching a college baseball game. The women, Leigh, Beth and Emma, were in the kitchen, supposedly doing the dishes. Joe figured they were comparing babies and their care, since he hadn't heard any dishes clink together in quite a while.

A knock on the door brought Jack to his feet. "You think this is Ryan?"

"I don't think so. Leigh called today to invite him, but Billy said he already had plans."

"A new woman?" Jack asked, frowning.

"No!" Joe insisted with a scowl.

Jack opened the door. "Steve! Come on in." He stepped back to let the doctor enter. Then he remembered his wife had seen him that morning. "Did you find something wrong? Is the baby or Beth sick?"

"No, Jack, everything's fine with Beth and your son is a bruiser with a powerful set of lungs."

Jack grinned, happy with that report.

"But there is a problem." Steve hurriedly added, "Not with the babies or Beth or Emma."

Joe stood. "Need me to leave the room?"

"No, Joe, you're the reason I'm here."

"You found something wrong with Leigh? What is it? Is it serious?" Joe grabbed Steve's arm in a death grip.

"Easy, Joe, that arm used to work."

Joe backed off, staring at Steve.

"It's not Leigh, Joe. It's your son."

"Ryan? Ryan's not sick."

Steve took a deep breath. "When was the last time you saw him?"

Jack stepped closer. "Something's wrong with Ryan?"

"I just had dinner with him. He's lost at least ten pounds this past week. His cheeks are gaunt, he's pale."

"Maybe he's got the flu. Did you check him out?" Joe asked.

"At the café? No. I asked if he needed to come to the office, but he wasn't interested. That's why I'm here. I figure you're the only one who can get him to come in."

Joe rubbed his chin. "I don't know. He's been working himself to death, according to Billy. But I'll try. I'll go out tomorrow and talk to him."

"Don't wait any longer than that," Steve warned.

"He's that bad?"

"I'm afraid he'll come down with something. His resistance can't be very good."

Satisfied that Joe finally understood how serious the situation could become, Steve said his goodnights and left.

Leigh poked her head out of the kitchen. "Did I hear a door? Is someone here?"

"Come here, Leigh," Joe said.

She turned back to tell the girls she'd return in a minute. Then she came into the den. One look at her husband's face and she grew alarmed. "What's wrong?"

"That was Steve. He dropped by to ask me to talk to Ryan."

"About Emma? There's nothing wrong with Emma, is there? She said Steve told her she was doing well."

"There's nothing wrong with Emma. It's Ryan."

"Ryan's sick? Don't be ridiculous. He's never sick. Why, he's as strong as a horse."

"Apparently he's not sleeping or eating."

Leigh's eyes rounded. "Oh, no," she whispered. "It's like when Merilee and the baby died. Steve got him to take something to get him to sleep. Why didn't he just—"

"Ryan says there's nothing wrong."

"What are we going to do?" Leigh asked, her lips quivering as she ran into her husband's arms.

"I'm going to talk to him tomorrow. I'll get him to go. Everything will be all right, honey, I promise."

The kitchen door opened and Emma and Beth came into the room.

"What's wrong?" Beth asked immediately.

"Nothing," Joe said gruffly, still comforting his wife.

The obvious lie brought Emma forward. "If you need to talk without me here, I can—"

Leigh turned around wiping her eyes. "Don't be silly, Emma, dear. I was just—it's—you tell them, Joe."

"Uh, Ryan's a little under the weather."

Emma's heart started beating overtime as fear spread through her.

Chapter Twelve

"What's wrong with Ryan, Joe?" Emma demanded, almost holding her breath until he answered.

"He's going to be okay, Emma. But he's not eating or sleeping much right now. Steve's worried about him. We think…that is…he's upset about everything."

"What can I do?" she asked, ready to spring into action. She didn't want Ryan to suffer. He'd done nothing wrong.

"Nothing, honey," Joe said, patting her on the shoulder. "I'm going to go talk to him in the morning."

"I'm going with you," she said, not bothering to ask.

"Now, Emma, that's not necessary."

"Yes, Joe, it is. This is all my fault," Emma said, feeling guilty. Here she was enjoying Ryan's family while he stood alone.

Leigh stepped forward. "Honey, what I think Joe is trying to say is that, if you go, it might give Ryan false hope."

"False hope?" Emma asked, not quite sure what Leigh meant.

"He might think you love him. He might think you're coming back to him."

"He doesn't want me, Leigh. I love him, but he doesn't want me." She bit her bottom lip to keep them from noticing its trembling.

Joe and Leigh looked at each other. Then Joe said, "I think you and Ryan got your wires crossed. Why do you think he's not eating or sleeping?"

Emma couldn't answer. She didn't want to express the hope that was causing her heart to beat faster. She couldn't let herself believe that Ryan loved her. Instead of answering Joe's question, she said, "I have to go with you."

"It will be early," Joe warned.

She nodded.

Beth stepped forward. "Why don't you and Andy spend the night here? Then I'll keep Andy while you go out to the ranch. As long as you're back here by eight to feed her, everything will be all right."

"You don't mind?" Emma asked.

"No. I want you and Ryan to work things out," Beth insisted with a hug. "You're the sister I never had."

Emma's eyes filled with tears and she sniffed.

"Come on," Joe said. "I'll drive you to your place to get a change of clothes and things for Andy."

* * *

The sun was just coming up when Joe, Leigh and Emma pulled up beside the ranch house. There were several lights already on.

"Looks like he's up," Joe said. "Better let me go first. Who knows what kind of shape he's in."

Leigh and Emma remained silent but followed Joe from the car. Leigh reached out and clasped hands with Emma. They both knew how important this morning could be.

Emma hadn't slept much the night before, trying to decide what she should do. If Ryan wanted her—she'd promised herself she wouldn't marry him if he didn't love her. But if he wanted her so badly he was making himself sick... She didn't know what to do.

She knew she wanted him, loved him. Wanted him to be Andy's daddy.

It all depended on...on what happened this morning.

Joe rapped sharply on the back door, then opened it and went in.

"Hi, Dad," Ryan greeted him.

"Damn, boy, what's the matter with you?" Joe said with a gasp. "You're skin and bones!"

"See, I told you," Billy said.

Emma held her breath, anxious to see just how bad off Ryan was, her tender heart eager to tend to him.

"Stop riding me, Billy," Ryan snapped.

"Have you eaten breakfast?" Joe asked. "Coffee is all you're having?"

Billy spoke again. "I keep telling him he's got to eat. And sleep, too. He's been wandering the house all night for the past week."

Emma couldn't wait any longer. She entered the kitchen, Leigh on her heels.

When she saw the man she'd always considered incredibly handsome, she gasped.

He turned to discover her there.

"Maybe you're right, Dad, 'cause now I'm seeing Emma when she isn't there," he said, his voice weary and hollow.

Softly she said, "I'm here, Ryan. You're not seeing things."

He froze, then said, "Why?"

"I was worried about you. Why are you doing this to yourself?"

He shook his head. "I don't know what you mean."

"You haven't been eating or sleeping. Why?"

"I can't—I'm worried about you and Andy. Is everything all right?" He took a step forward.

"We're fine." Her heart was full, and her eyes filled with tears. Maybe he couldn't love her, but he cared about her. And she knew he would love Andy. Had she asked too much? Could she accept what he offered?

She'd be a fool if she didn't, she decided. She loved him, and it looked like that was a permanent condition.

She cleared her throat. "Billy, can you fix us all breakfast while I get Ryan cleaned up? And Joe, can you call his manager and tell him Ryan won't be working today?"

Both men were staring at her with startled gazes, but they immediately agreed.

"What's going on? I don't want anything to eat. I don't feel so well. But I'm going to work," Ryan insisted, looking confused.

Instead of arguing, Emma held out her hand. "Come with me, Ryan."

"Emma—Emma I can't promise what you want. I can't just forget about Merilee and Ryan, Jr. I tried to—I can't. I looked at the photo albums. Billy showed me where you added the last of the pictures. I appreciate that. And maybe I've been obsessive about everything, but I can't just pretend they didn't exist."

It was as if Ryan was holding up a mirror for Emma. Guilt filled her. He hadn't understood her any more than she'd understood him. "Oh, Ryan," she said with a sigh. "I didn't mean you should forget either of them."

"You didn't?"

She gave him a watery smile. "Come on, we'll talk later. First you need to eat and sleep."

He frowned and stared at her hand. Finally he reached out to touch her and she breathed a sigh of relief. "Give us about twenty minutes, Billy."

"You got it."

She led Ryan up the stairs, hoping the dazed look on his face was because of shock at seeing her and not his physical state.

When they reached his room, she gently pushed him ahead of her. "I want you in the shower, Ryan. Then I want you to shave." He had about three days' growth on his face, making him look like a homeless man. "You'll feel better."

"Emma, did you hear what I said? I can't do what you asked."

She wrapped her arms around his waist and stood on tiptoe to kiss him briefly. "Ryan, I didn't mean that. Everything's going to be all right. If you don't mind, Andy and I are going to move back in. Only this time *I'm* going to take care of *you*. When we're both well again, we'll decide what to do."

"I don't want you to leave again, Emma. I can't stand this yo-yo stuff," he exclaimed, holding her tightly against him.

"I know. I'm here to stay if you want me."

He almost collapsed with relief.

"Don't fall asleep yet, Ryan!" Emma exclaimed. "Into the shower."

Like an obedient child, he headed for the shower in the connecting bath. When he stepped in, Emma realized she'd left out a step in the directions. "No, Ryan!"

He stopped and stared at her. "What?"

"Take off your clothes first."

With a frown, he swayed, holding on to the shower door. "Oh, yeah."

"Do you need any help?"

Her offer seemed to pierce his daze more than her earlier words had. "You're staying?"

She smiled at him. "I'm staying, I promise."

With a nod, he closed the door and, she hoped, undressed for his shower.

While he was cleaning up, she stripped the bed and found fresh sheets to put on it. When he opened the door a few minutes later, he looked much better, though still gaunt and exhausted.

"Do you want to eat breakfast downstairs or up here in bed?"

"Where will you be?"

"Wherever you are," she assured him.

"I'll eat downstairs, I guess. That will be less trouble."

She took his hand again, afraid he might collapse, and led him back to the kitchen.

"You're looking better, boy," Billy said as they came through the door. "Everything's ready."

Emma saw Ryan look at the food without comprehension. If he hadn't eaten much in a while, it would be difficult for him. She squeezed his hand. "Just try a little, Ryan."

He stared at her, his eyes a beautiful blue. "You're staying?"

"I'm staying."

She heard a gasp from one of his parents, probably Leigh, but she didn't turn around. Her attention was focused on Ryan.

He sat down beside her at the table, still holding her hand. The others joined them, but Emma asked Billy to get some milk for Ryan. "He doesn't need any more caffeine right now."

"A 'course. I should've thought of that."

"Milk?" Ryan said with a frown.

"That's what Andy and I get right now. I think you should drink milk in support, don't you?" She smiled and leaned over to brush his lips with hers.

"Uh, okay," he agreed, still staring at her.

Billy set the glass of milk in front of him and he picked it up and took a drink.

"Good, now let's eat some eggs. You have to have protein, you know," Emma suggested. She picked up her fork with the hand Ryan wasn't holding and took a bite of egg. Then she stared at him.

He did the same.

Leigh sighed and Billy and Joe relaxed.

"Ooh, the bacon's perfect, Billy. You're so good at cooking bacon, isn't he, Ryan?"

Ryan stared at her, and Emma wondered if he was understanding anything she said. He was more zombie than person. She picked up a piece of his bacon and held it to his lips.

He took a bite and chewed, and Emma was cheered. After he ate, she'd tuck him in bed. When he'd had some sleep, he'd start to act more like his normal self. Then she could be sure he wanted her to stay.

"Where's Andy?" he suddenly asked.

"She's with Beth," Leigh said. She looked at her watch. "Emma has to be back there by eight o'clock."

"You said you'd stay," Ryan said, alarm in his voice.

"I'm going to. But I have to pick up Andy and bring her here. You don't mind if she comes too, do you?" Emma held her breath. If sex was all he wanted, then Andy wouldn't matter.

"This is Andy's home. Of course she comes here. You promise?"

She leaned over and brushed his lips with hers

again, enjoying the freedom to touch him. "I promise. I think she's missed you."

He smiled, but as he did so, his eyelids began to sag.

"Ryan," she said, shaking his arm, "you need to eat a little more before you go to sleep. Okay?"

He managed a couple more bites of scrambled eggs and another piece of bacon. Then he smiled at Emma even as he wavered in the chair. "Need to sleep. Promise?"

She understood him perfectly and nodded again. "I promise."

"Andy, too?"

"Definitely Andy, too."

As if satisfied, he closed his eyes.

"Wait! Joe, we need to get him upstairs."

His father and Billy got on each side of him and urged him to his feet. Emma ran ahead of them and turned down the sheets. Leigh brought up the rear, hovering over her son.

Joe helped Emma peel the shirt off Ryan. Then he undid the jeans and after Ryan fell on the bed, he slid them off him. Only his underwear remained.

Emma pulled the cover up over him. Then she turned to her assistants. "Thanks for helping. I'm going to stay a few minutes to be sure he gets to sleep. Then I'll be down and we can go back to town."

The other three backed through the door, Joe giving her a thumbs-up signal and Leigh beaming.

Emma sat down on the edge of the bed, running her fingers through Ryan's hair. For the first time in many months, she could touch him as she pleased. Even back then, when they'd been lovers, he hadn't drawn close. But now, he was going to be her husband. He might not love her as she wanted, but he wanted her.

She'd thought she was doing the right thing when she'd demanded he love her. But she hadn't meant he had to forget about his first wife and child.

How was she going to make that clear to Ryan? How was she going to assure him she had no intention of taking his family away from him?

She stared around the room, trying to think.

Then she had an idea.

Emma found Ryan's family ready to do whatever she asked. She'd never had the support and love of a family before, and she wanted to pinch herself every five minutes to be sure she was awake.

"I'm so glad," Beth exclaimed, when Leigh told her Emma and Ryan were going to be married.

Emma smiled but cautioned, "We have to wait until he's coherent to be sure. I think if I'd asked him to rob a bank today, he would've asked which bank. He was like a zombie."

"Well, I'm sure," Leigh protested. "How soon shall we plan the wedding?"

"Well, there won't be all that much planning to do," Emma pointed out. "We won't have a big wedding."

Before Leigh could protest, as it was obvious she intended to, Joe said, "If you think we're going to let the two of you marry as if you're ashamed of what you're doing, you're crazy, Emma Davenport. We've got a lot to celebrate.''

"If Ryan agrees.''

"He'll agree,'' Joe said, grinning.

"Okay. I guess I can use my savings,'' she muttered to herself.

"You'll do no such thing!'' Leigh exclaimed. "Joe and I will give you the wedding as your gift. Or think of us as your parents, because after the wedding, we will be your parents.''

"But—'' Emma began, embarrassed because traditionally the bride's family paid for the wedding.

Beth hugged her. "You might as well give in, Emma. You're a member of our family now, and it's time you realized how stubborn we Nixes are.''

"We'll discuss the wedding after Ryan agrees to it,'' Emma finally said. "Can you take me to the apartment?'' she asked Joe. "I want to be sure I'm at the ranch when he wakes up.''

Joe agreed, though he pointed out that it was only a little after eight-thirty. "I think he'll sleep at least twelve hours.''

"I know, but I want to be sure.''

"I'll come with you two and help you pack, dear,'' Leigh said.

"Thank you,'' Emma said. "Of course, I've done this several times. I should be an expert by now.''

"That's a knowledge you won't be needing again,'' Joe said firmly. "After all, I heard you promise Ryan.''

She nodded. "If that's what he wants.'' Then she went to pick up Andy, already back asleep.

"Like father like daughter," she murmured, a smile on her face.

Emma took care of her secret plan while she was in town, and the store clerk promised to have it ready by five o'clock. She'd see if Billy could pick it up.

Then she drove herself and Andy to the ranch. Joe and Leigh offered to come with her, but she refused. Billy could help her unload.

"Do you think we could move Andy's nursery to the second floor, Billy? I can climb the stairs okay now, as long as I don't hurry."

"Sure can." Billy beamed from ear to ear, as he'd done ever since Emma arrived back at the house. He'd showed his pleasure at her return.

"Maybe I should wait until I talk to Ryan after he wakens," Emma mused out loud. While his family seemed sure he had known what he was saying, Emma wasn't.

"That's not necessary. We'll get you all settled in while he's sleeping. He'll be pleased."

"I hope you're right."

Emma took a nap that afternoon. In Ryan's bed. He hadn't moved since she'd tucked him in earlier, but there was plenty of room left over for her. And it felt so good to sleep next to him.

When Andy woke her at four, right on schedule for her afternoon feeding, Ryan's arm was looped over her, holding her close, as if, in sleep, he was showing his approval.

She hoped that was what he was doing.

Easing his arm back, she slid out of the bed and hurried to her demanding child right next door. "Hi, sweetie. Are you hungry? Daddy's going to be glad you're here, when he wakes up. But if you keep on screaming, he might change his mind." She was teasing, she hoped, but she hurriedly gave Andy what she wanted. Then Emma relaxed in the rocker, enjoying the special time with her baby.

Could she really expect such a happy ending? Or was it too perfect to be true? She'd be married to the man she loved, living in the midst of a loving family, raising their daughter.

"Please, God, let it be true," she whispered.

When she went downstairs after feeding Andy, she found a package on the kitchen table.

"I picked up that package. What's in it?" Billy asked.

"A surprise for Ryan," she said, but she refused to reveal anything else. She hoped she was doing the right thing.

"Think he's going to wake up for dinner?"

"I'm not sure, Billy. If he's had as little sleep as you've said, he might not. But he needs to eat. Maybe I can wake him up enough to feed him."

When Billy had the food ready, Emma fixed a tray with more milk and the steak, potatoes and beans Billy had fixed. "I'll be back in a few minutes," she assured him.

Upstairs, she struggled to get Ryan awake. Finally, after calling his name and shaking him, she piled a couple of pillows behind him. "Ryan, I want you to eat dinner. Are you awake?"

"Uh-uh." He rolled to his side.

She finally did the only thing she thought he'd respond to. She kissed him.

That got his attention. His eyes fluttered open. "Emma? I'm not dreaming?"

"No, you're not dreaming. But you need to eat a little something. Then you can go back to sleep."

"And you'll be here when I wake up?" he asked, his frown in place.

"Right beside you. Here, open up." She put a forkful of food in his mouth. "Chew!" she ordered, since his eyes were closing.

He chewed.

She tried the glass of milk next, knowing she didn't have long. He managed about five more bites and the glass of milk before he flopped over, his eyes firmly shut.

But Emma was worried. She'd moved back in, and Ryan didn't even realize he'd agreed. What if when he woke he was angry and threw her out?

If he did, she was leaving town at once.

His parents were planning a wedding.

Reaching out her hand, she caressed his cheek. All she could do was wait...and hope.

Ryan's stomach growling woke him the next morning. His first thought was that he was feeling better than he had in a while. His second was that life looked better today.

His third was that someone was in his bed.

His eyes popped open and he looked at Emma's peaceful face on the pillow next to him. Emma! He vaguely remembered her and his parents coming to the ranch. But what had happened for her to end up in his bed? Had he promised the impossible—to forget Merilee and his son?

If he had, he'd have to be honest with her today. She might leave, and the pain would be even greater. He'd finally admitted to himself that he loved her and Andy. Somewhere in that fog in which he'd lived, that idea had come out. Maybe he didn't have to tell her that he'd still think about his first family.

If he didn't tell her, she'd think he was doing what she wanted. Would that be so bad? He'd have her and Andy with him, a second chance at a family.

It wouldn't be honest.

He was considering reaching out to touch her, when his daughter let out a scream. Andy! Before he could get out of bed to fetch his daughter, Emma opened her eyes.

"Good morning, Ryan. I guess our daughter is ready to have breakfast. Are you?"

"Emma! Uh, yeah."

She was already making her way out of bed, dressed in a thin cotton nightgown that brought him fully awake. "I'll be right back."

Was she going to bring Andy in here to feed her? Was he finally going to get to watch Emma nurse the baby? He'd longed to share that experience with her.

He heard her voice. "Billy, breakfast in half an hour, please?"

"You got it!" Billy roared back.

Then she appeared in the door with a whimpering

Andy. "She's not very patient, is she? Billy says she gets that from you. He said Ryan, Jr., was the same way."

He was stunned by her mentioning his son. He stared at her as she returned to the bed. Until she landed Andy in his lap.

"Can you hold her while I pile up some pillows?"

"Uh, sure," he muttered, a little confused about Emma's behavior.

She settled in the bed, leaning on him, and arranged her gown to expose one breast. Then she took the baby from him, and he watched his tiny daughter latch on to Emma's breast as if she were starving to death.

She looked up. "If you don't want to be here for Miss Piggy's breakfast, I'm sure Billy has some coffee ready."

"No! No, I want to watch. But I don't think you should call this sweet baby a pig."

She chuckled. "If you were the one breast-feeding her, I think you'd agree."

They sat in silence after he slipped an arm around her shoulders. Holding the two of them close to him filled him with contentment.

When she needed to change breasts, Emma asked Ryan to burp Andy while she got ready. He rubbed and patted Andy's little back, still amazed at how small she was, until she produced a large burp.

Emma laughed again and took her daughter back. "Good to have an expert around," she said. "How long did it take Ryan, Jr., to sleep all night? I meant to ask Dr. Lambert, but I forgot."

"Emma—I don't understand."

"What?"

He didn't want to have a discussion now. He was just inside the door of paradise, but he couldn't continue until they talked.

"Why are you talking about—about my son?"

She acted as if she hadn't heard him, staring at Andy as she ate. Just as he was about to ask his question again, she looked up at him. "I wanted you to know I made a mistake."

"About what?"

"I didn't make it clear what I wanted."

He frowned. "Tell me now."

"I didn't mean you had to forget Merilee and Ryan, Jr. I know you loved them and always will. All I wanted was for you to let us in, too."

Tears filled his eyes, and he wrapped her into his embrace, along with Andy. He laid his head on hers and said a prayer of thanks. "I do love you. I love Andy."

"Then everything's all right? You still want us to stay?"

"Of course I do!" he exclaimed, pulling back. "You had doubts?"

"I wasn't sure you were aware of what you were saying yesterday morning. I didn't want to assume— you were pretty out of it."

"What did I say?"

"You said you wanted me to stay."

"I hope I added forever?"

She shook her head no.

He leaned down and kissed her, a deep, satisfying

kiss. When he raised his head, he said, "When did Steve say you could—you know?"

"I didn't ask. There didn't seem like there were any prospects of—you know—when I saw him." She tilted her head. "Besides, I think you may not be ready for that yet. You were pretty weak last night."

Before he could answer, Andy pushed away from Emma, her tummy full. "Burping duties again," Emma said, handing Andy to him.

"I like this shared stuff."

"Me, too," she assured him with that brilliant smile again.

"Breakfast!" Billy called up the stairs.

"We'll be right there," Emma said. Then, as Andy burped, she said. "You'd better give her to me and put some pants on. We don't want to shock Billy."

"Are you going down like that?" he asked.

"No, I'm going to wear the robe my wonderful hus—I mean, you bought me at the hospital."

"You can call me husband. We will be soon enough," he assured her.

"Oh, good, then I can tell you your mother is already planning it."

"That's fine, as long as it's soon." He got out of bed, surprised to find his legs a little shaky. He crossed to the dresser to find a pair of jeans. As he opened the second drawer, his gaze fell on a portrait, nicely framed, sitting on top.

It hadn't been there before.

After Merilee's and his son's deaths, he'd removed all the pictures. He couldn't bear the sight of them.

But his favorite picture of the three of them now occupied a place of honor on the dresser.

"Emma? Where did this come from?" he asked, his voice cracking.

Having shrugged into her robe, Emma, with Andy in her arms, joined him. "I hope you don't mind. I thought—I thought it would show you that I'm not trying to shut them out. We're all family now."

He wrapped his arms around her and the baby, his gaze still on the picture. "I believe you, sweetheart, but I appreciate your putting the picture there." He kissed her forehead. "Are you sure you don't mind?"

"Never."

Ryan held her closer against him. Finally, he had his family again. All of them.

"These eggs are getting cold!" Billy yelled.

"Are you okay?" Emma whispered.

"Yeah, I'm okay, for the first time in a long time."

"Then we'd better go fatten you up so people won't think I'm a horrible cook when we get married."

They went down the stairs arm-in-arm—as they would always be.

* * * * *

Don't miss the reprisal of
Silhouette Romance's popular miniseries

When King Michael of Edenbourg goes missing, his devoted family and loyal subjects make it their mission to bring him home safely!

Royally Wed

The Stanbury Crown

Their search begins March 2001 and continues through June 2001.

On sale March 2001: **THE EXPECTANT PRINCESS** by bestselling author **Stella Bagwell** (SR #1504)

On sale April 2001: **THE BLACKSHEEP PRINCE'S BRIDE** by rising star **Martha Shields** (SR #1510)

On sale May 2001: **CODE NAME: PRINCE** by popular author **Valerie Parv** (SR #1516)

On sale June 2001: **AN OFFICER AND A PRINCESS** by award-winning author **Carla Cassidy** (SR #1522)

Available at your favorite retail outlet.

Silhouette ®
Where love comes alive ™

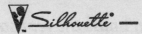

RX PRESCRIPTION ROMANCE

Get swept away by
these warmhearted romances featuring
dedicated doctors and nurses....

LOVE IS JUST
A HEARTBEAT AWAY!

Available in April 2001 at your favorite retail outlet:

HOLDING THE BABY
by Laura MacDonald

TENDER LIAISON
by Joanna Neil

A FAMILIAR FEELING
by Margaret Barker

HEAVEN SENT
by Carol Wood

MAITLAND MATERNITY

Where the luckiest babies are born!

In May 2001 look for

GUARDING CAMILLE
by Judy Christenberry

**He promised to watch over her—
day and night....**

Jake Maitland, FBI agent and black sheep of the Maitland
clan, had finally come home. And he had a whole lot
of trouble on his tail....

Camille Eckart was Jake's latest assignment. He'd been
chosen as her protector, to keep her safe from her mobster
ex-husband. Only, little did he guess that Camille's main
objective was to make Jake see her not as a case,
but as a woman....

Silhouette®
Where love comes alive™

HARLEQUIN®
Makes any time special ™

Visit us at www.eHarlequin.com   MMCNM-9